The Hollywood Sisters

caught on tape

The Hollywood Sisters

backstage pass

on location

caught on tape

The Hollywood Sisters

caught on tape

Mary Wilcox

DELACORTE PRESS

J Wilcox

Published by Delacorte Press
an imprint of Random House Children's Books
a division of Random House, Inc.
New York

www.randomhouse.com/teens

Educators and librarians, for a variety of teaching tools,
visit us at www.randomhouse.com/teachers

Library of Congress Cataloging-in-Publication Data
Wilcox, Mary.
Caught on tape / Mary Wilcox.—1st ed.
p. cm.—(The Hollywood sisters)
Summary: A broken heart, an intrusive public, and a streak of bad luck
convince Jess that being the younger sister of a major television star has
its drawbacks.
ISBN: 978-0-385-73356-4 (trade pbk.)
ISBN: 978-0-385-90371-4 (glb)
[1. Actors and actresses—Fiction. 2. Sisters—Fiction. 3. Family life—Fiction.
4. Hollywood (Los Angeles, Calif.)—Fiction.] I. Title II. Series: Wilcox, Mary.
Hollywood sisters.
PZ7.W64568Cau 2007
[Fic] 22
2006026508

Printed in the United States of America

10 9 8 7 6 5 4 3 2 1

First Edition

For an all-star brother, Michael Hogan

MY SISTER TELLS ME NOT TO OBSESS,
BUT I WANT TO GET THE TRUTH OUT THERE. SO HERE ARE THE
TOP FIVE HOLLYWOOD LIES—I HOPE YOU CAN SEE THEM
COMING BETTER THAN I DID:

★ I eat anything I want.

★ I never work out.

★ I'm so over the whole nightclub scene.

★ Fame is just the price I have to pay for
my art.

AND THE ONE THAT REALLY BITES MY BUTT:

★ I didn't steal him.

Act I

There are girls, people in the industry, who just kind of flip through magazines and pick out guys, like, "I'm gonna date him." I could never do that. I don't think being set up works. I'm big into fate.

—KATE BOSWORTH

The August sunset reflects off the rims of my mom's car. Perhaps you've seen it around Beverly Hills? It's the one that's not a Lexus/Prius/Status vehicle; it's a Why Us?

Why are we driving around a thousand-year-old Nissan Maxima?

Because we can, my dad would answer. It's because of his super-mechanic skills that the car looks ancient from the outside but is all new under the hood.

Woo-freaking-hoo.

It's a strange feeling to follow my sister's exploding acting career from our little house in Anaheim to this mansion in the Hills, and then watch the gardeners roll up in a better ride. (The neighbors once left a note asking if we could park the car around back—though the handwriting looked a lot like Eva's.)

Eva and I share a look as we pass the Maxima. We are taking my dog, Petunia, for a walk.

Before you get too impressed that Eva Ortiz, sixteen-year-old breakout star of ABC's hit sitcom *Two Sisters* and Young Latina of the Year, still makes time for walks with her little sister, listen in on her warm, cheery conversation: "So tell me about getting your heart broken into teeny-tiny pieces, Jess. Was it a sharp, stabbing pain? Or a slow, rolling agony?"

She's one big warm fuzzy, isn't she?

Eva sweeps her long dark hair back from her face. She gets described as a sweeter-looking Jessica Alba (as in, you could leave your bf alone in the room with her), but I can't see what all the fuss is about. One day she was just, you know, Eva—taking up Mom's time driving to auditions, and taking up our bedroom with her bursting closet—and the next, she was someone that people had opinions about. Her hair, her weight, her Latina-ness—all discussed in magazines. By grown-ups. Seriously.

What if they could hear her now?

"Is there a moment in the morning when you think you're happy, then feel doubly crushed to remember you're miserable?"

I feel like doubly crushing something right now. "Who says I'm miserable?"

"Well, you thought you had a chance with Jeremy Jones—until Paige was all over him like a fake tan."

Is Eva missing the sensitivity chip?

Yep, almost entirely.

Though in this case, she's quizzing me because her character on the show is about to get dumped. E has only been on the "handing out" side of heartache, so she needs my valuable life experience to draw from. She's fully wielding her impressions notebook—part of an acting technique where she writes down the details of strong emotional states for future reference.

"C'mon, Jess, you've hardly said a word about Jeremy to me."

"That's because I'm ignoring you."

"Oh. Well, you're not very good at it."

Grrr . . .

"But seriously . . ." When Eva's mad at me, it's serious, and when I'm mad at her, it's a joke. Life as a little sister. "Talking things out can help."

"Is that what you told Mom when you said you'd walk Petunia with me?" Little P is a great dog, a black, white, and brown English bulldog. She's rocking the "small but not yappy" mojo.

"Mom thinks I'm giving you a pep talk about starting at your new school. So . . . school. Go to it."

"Wow, look out, ninth grade. I feel completely pepped now. Thanks."

E smiles. "They're lucky to have you. What's to talk about?"

Our driveway opens onto a narrow road. The houses in Beverly Hills are huge but packed close. As we make our way slowly down and around the climbing street, we see the red tops of the Spanish villas, tucked behind gates and gardens. It's dangerously steep—one misstep and we're walking on top of someone's roof.

Looking out over the view, Eva squeezes my arm. "Jess, really . . . are you okay?"

E's concern calls for a sisterly response. I stick my tongue out at her.

She holds up her hands. "Okay, okay! But I wish you'd open up a little. Mom says you don't even show her your poetry anymore."

I picked up a bad habit from my mom. No, it's not her librarian's love of organizing clothes by the Dewey decimal system ("Look, the Versace dresses are under 391 for Fashion, Italian!"). It's her habit of writing rhymes. My fingers crumple around the scrap in my pocket.

We ditched our old life
(Except for our car)
When we zoomed like the tail
On E's flying star.

I'm working through
What it's all about;
A recovering shy girl—
I watch/listen/help out.

I'm at private school soon,
All plaid skirts and pearls,
Let's hope it's not packed
Wall-to-wall with mean girls!

As we walk, Petunia rubs her back against the bumpy stucco walls. The black eyes of the not-so-hidden cameras whir her way.

There are two types of houses in my neighborhood—million-dollar mansions and piles of rubble. Weird, but true. If you're new to the neighborhood, you plunk down big bucks for a flash pad, then call in contractors to wrecking-ball the place. Then you build your dream mansion. Which you quickly sell to someone else—who comes in and wrecking-balls the place. You're not upset because you have moved on to destroying a bigger, better house.

Eva and I are the only people around. A walk-the-dog neighborhood it's not.

My thoughts are drifting, so I'm surprised when Eva jerks me and Little P off the road moments before an open-topped gold bus whips round the corner. The bus is old, bulky, and packed with tourists taking snapshots in the open air. The guide is also the driver. One hand is on the wheel, one on his microphone. Both feet seem to be standing on the gas.

The speaker blares: "Coming up on our right will be the home of Eva Ortiz, the *Two Sisters* star! Let's give her the Golden Tours welcome to the neighborhood!"

An air horn blasts and the tourists shout: "Golden Girl! Golden Girl!"

Yikes. Nothing says "good neighbor" like attracting a screaming, speeding bus of gawking strangers to the hood. Class-ee.

Moving to Beverly Hills means that I live in a town where Jackie Chan shares a street with Diddy and Kathy Bates. But I've never spotted a sightseeing bus around here—our road is way too windy and narrow. And the buses I've seen in other parts of town were discreet, slow-moving, and small. And not trying to kill me.

As Eva and I stare at the bus—it drives right onto our property!

It spins around the circular driveway and back out to the street—air horn blasting!

That's not right!

I scoop Petunia up and we all stumble home, choking on a thick cloud of Golden exhaust. I guess there's a reason no one walks in L.A.

Scene 2

FADE IN.

EXTERIOR SHOT: EARLY-MORNING SUNSHINE LIGHTS THE SMOG OVER LOS ANGELES. CAMERA PULLS IN CLOSER TOWARD A LARGE WHITE VILLA. BLACK LIMOUSINE PURRS AT THE FRONT DOOR.

CUT TO: PLUSH INTERIOR OF LIMO. FOUR FEMALES.

A few years ago, Mom took Eva on some commercial auditions because a friend and her son were going. His mom was the one who said things like: "If you get a callback, I'll take you to McDonald's!" And mine was the one who said, "Just have fun."

How did it all work out?

They're back in Anaheim now, with nothing to show for their trouble except bruised egos. But Eva? The camera *loved* Eva. And the affection was mutual.

What started out as a lark has turned into a full-blown celebrity lifestyle, complete with a twenty-four-year-old publicist in knee-high boots and a chartreuse minidress who plans Eva's day like it's an attack on a neighboring village.

"Good morning, Eva! You look a mile beyond fabulous! Marc Jacobs was dreaming of you when he designed those pants!"

Okay. I admit it's an incredibly *perky* attack on a neighboring village.

As usual, Keiko is waiting in the limo that arrives to pick up E, Mom, and me. She says there's news I won't want to miss, but she doesn't tell me what. Her dark eyes are smiling under her razor-cut platinum hair. As a publicist, Keiko's job is to manage Eva's image in the media. Part of that job seems to be knowing everything that's going to happen before it happens.

Mom keeps her voice light. "Keiko, there's not going to be a surprise guest star, is there?"

"No, nothing like that. Besides, Jessica's bad-luck streak is sure to end sometime."

The history of me and the show's guest stars . . . how can I put this?

Plaid/polka dots.

Orange juice/pizza.

Honesty/publicity.

Bad/mix.

As far as my luck changing, I hope this is one more time when Keiko knows something before the rest of the world.

I look through the pile of magazines scattered across the seat. Jeremy and Paige have been getting a lot more coverage since people started wondering if they were dating. Eva is flipping through the *Hollywood Reporter*. She points to a movie ad with her favorite actress. "She looks great. Lost all that baby weight."

"Her?" Keiko raises an eyebrow. "Please. She's on the Photoshop Diet. You should see her when her head is on her own body." Keiko looks right at me and winks. "You can't believe everything you see in this town."

We pull onto the set. What does Keiko know that I don't?

There's a lot that's cool about being on the set of a major TV show. The smells of sawdust, fresh paint, and cinnamon rolls from the Craft Services buffet. The warmth of the bright lights. The look of the stage—exactly like the exposed back of a life-sized dollhouse.

But you won't like the place if you can't stand the spin.

Spin control, that is.

The usual *Two Sisters* plots involve "sisters" Lavender and Paige, plus their neighbors, Eva and Jeremy, acting like regular Boston high school students by day while taking on a petnapping ring at night. The show was pitched as "What does America love more than reality contests? Cute girls and puppies!"

Every week, cast and crew work to bring twenty-two minutes of story to your screen.

But backstage? The drama *never* stops.

Take the latest: Last Thursday, with blond hair flying and green eyes fluttering, Paige screamed that she had gotten hurt on set. No one had seen exactly what happened, but hysteria and a hospital visit followed. She got a ton of attention—and she seemed to need Jeremy Jones by her side for every minute of it.

But she forgot one thing. Even when no one is watching, eyes can be on you. The eyes of the cameras.

Today the news is buzzing from the props room to the wardrobe closets: when the lawyers worried that Paige was going to sue the studio, they hit Rewind and Replay on every camera on set . . . and there was Paige, slowly lowering herself to the floor. Careful not to wrinkle her skirt.

She faked the whole thing!

She was never hurt!

Now, what would happen to you if you pulled a stunt like that? If you got everyone all worried, took up the time of busy ER doctors, and stopped work for an afternoon? What if you did all that just to get attention? And to keep a guy by your side?

Would your friends and family be incredibly . . . *impressed*?

Yeah, mine neither.

But in the life of a TV star . . . "Paige, your total-immersion acting technique is incredibly *impressive*!"

Hold on.

The set is about to start spinning.

"Your commitment to your craft is absolute!" Paige's agent is talking to anyone who will listen about how Paige's "accident" was arranged to help her completely dive into her character.

The agent is even trying to convince me while I cruise the breakfast buffet. "Paige keeps going to new places in her work. She's reaching new levels. Don't you agree?"

I almost choke on a cinnamon roll. "What about that little granny she wrestled for a wheelchair in the ER?"

The agent narrows her eyes. "New. Levels." She stomps off, looking for a better audience.

Lighting Guy Bob is at my side. "So the girl was never injured."

"Pretty surprising, huh?"

"Kind of." Bob shrugs. "Who knew Paige Carey could act?"

Scene 4

*A*cting—the job that makes you smile.

People on set aren't buying Paige's "new approach to her craft" as an excuse for her behavior. (The girl practically demanded piggyback rides to the stage!) But today is shoot day. That means: lights, camera, and smile-like-you-mean-it.

All week long the writers polish the script, the actors rehearse, and the technical crews prepare. Then on Friday, cast and crew get revved: the audience is coming.

These are the people who decide what shows up on your screen versus the editing room floor. The show is desperate for "real-world" viewers, and Los Angeles invites in a new batch every day: they're called tourists.

Security is leading in the first group, all of whom are already starting to shiver. That's right: bring a jacket if you're ever in a studio audience. Cold air will be blasting on you all afternoon to balance out the hot stage lights. And by "all afternoon," I mean the five or six hours it can take to get the show on tape.

Why so long for a half-hour sitcom? Mainly because you'll be seeing the show in order. Between scenes, the crew has to move cameras, set up lights, and deal with wardrobe changes. On taped shows, they film all the "living room" scenes at once, then all the "kitchen" scenes. But *Two Sisters* is a sitcom—a situation comedy. And what the producers want to know is: *Are you laughing at the situation?* If you don't laugh, the writing crew is standing by with backup jokes—or else with worried faces.

The first thing you notice when you see the set is that it's smaller than you expected. Every show has to make the most of its space, and set designers have come up with lots of ways to fool the eye, like the walls have angles built in to trick you into seeing depth; the set pieces closest to you are darker and larger, the ones in back lighter and smaller. And that view of "Boston Harbor" from the sisters' apartment? In person, you'll notice it looks a lot more like what it is: a massively blown-up digital photograph. (But wait till L.G. Bob turns on his theatrical lighting—it will seem like you could swim in the water.)

I'm seated in the VIP section with Mom and Keiko, and right next to one of the big stars from ABC. He's so familiar-looking, it's like he jumped out of a TV. I smile in a noncommittal "oh yeah, it's you" way. He returns a "yeah, but don't talk to me" nod. Around us, the audience pretends not to notice him while taking stealth pictures with their cell phones.

The first performer you'll see isn't a cast member, it's the audience entertainer. He'll ask where everyone is from, tell stories, and run contests—anything to build up excitement. He'll work between scenes, too, throwing out jokes and snacks. The show doesn't want your stomach growling into the mikes!

The cast comes out to wave—and yes, they look smaller than you expected too. The camera makes everything, and everyone, look bigger.

Then . . . action!

The first scene has the three actresses at the Boston Beanery. Onstage, extras are pouring sodas for Paige, Lavender, and Eva. (Oops, I'm not supposed to say "extras." The correct term now is "background." Is it the former shy girl in me, or is "background" an even worse way to refer to someone?)

It's no coincidence that the girls are drinking Zipps soda. Zipps has paid the price. If the drink sits on the table, they pay; if an actor drinks it, they pay more; and if the actor says he likes it, they pay most of all.

Paige has the first lines of dialogue, and she sounds choppy, off-key. They stop and reshoot again. And again.

It's an off night for her.

She is struggling. A lot.

As soon as I'm a much better person, I'm going to feel bad about that.

The script then calls for Lavender to get into a fight with the Beanery clerk over the song on the stereo. Lavender is working her usual end of the wardrobe rainbow in an indigo sundress with amethyst jewelry. She tosses her dark hair and narrows her violet eyes at the Beanery clerk. Then she reaches for the dial and pumps up the music, and . . . for a moment . . . no one notices that anything is wrong.

Really wrong.

Lavender is the first to catch on and she tries to turn off the stereo, but the knob breaks off in her hand, and now the song is blasting:

Lawyers say

Can't use your name

When I write this song

To complain about

You!

Purple liar!

You!

Purple cheat!

You!

Purple faker!

Your real name

Rhymes with scavenger!

I think it's actually "Lavenger" that rhymes with scavenger, but I get where the guy is going with this. I look at Lavender turning as purple as her signature color, and I realize: I'm not the only one who blunders when it comes to boys.

Lavender dated and dumped the songwriter for a band. She doesn't keep bfs around for long, but I thought maybe her last one had a chance. Besides his band, Runny Snots, Murphy also has his own TV show, the prank-pulling reality show *Crank Pranksters*, and an unbearably cocky attitude—if you like that sort of thing. But Lavender's loves seem to come stamped with an expiration date, and Murphy's came up quick.

It's hard to feel sorry for Lavender; she's a gorgeous brunette Southern belle who never remembers my name . . . but even I'm feeling the cringe for her as "Purple Heartache" plays.

I almost feel bad enough not to repeat the next part of the song. Which is:

Can't believe
I fell for your line
When you were making time
On the side.

You're a Georgia peach
All stuffed with flies.

(refrain repeats)

Onstage, the show's producer, Roman Capo, finally manages to disable the stereo, but at this point the audience has picked up the tune. And—*oh, no!*—it's singalong time!

Dozens of tourists belt out:

"You!
Purple liar!
You!
Purple cheat!
You!
Purple faker!"

Keiko elbows me. "Stop singing, Jessica."

Oops. Dozens of tourists plus me.

In my defense, the tune is completely catchy.

"Sorry, Keiko. Bad publicity?"

"No, you're rattling the fillings in my teeth." It's true. Bullfrogs sing better.

Roman gets the audience quieted, and shooting continues. Makeup covers up the angry violet splotches on Lavender's face, and the rest of the show goes smoothly. Then it's free pizza for the audience, who will get to hear their laughter on air when the show runs in six weeks.

The tourists only have to wait one day to see a mention of their afternoon in the Saturday edition of the local gossip column, Hollywood Hype.

Out of Tune

Can you guess which song, packed with purple prose, stopped shooting on the *Two Sisters* set? And who was the prankster behind the playback payback? Hint: Hype is *snot* telling.

For a blind item, anyone can see it means trouble ahead.

The weekend is supposed to mean a break from Hollywood madness. But not this Sunday.

My family is all piled into the car to go to church. We're pulling to the end of our driveway when we hear a Golden Tours bus. The guide is blaring his spiel through the speaker: ". . . home of Eva Ortiz! I only ever see the housekeepers exiting in an old car, but someday, we're sure to spot the star herself!"

Eva sinks down lower in her seat. Actually, so do Mom and I.

The bus zooms toward us, and Dad barely manages to swerve out of the way. Then he spins the Maxima back onto the property (thanks to his work, the vehicle has racecar-like responsiveness). He spits out a long string of words in which the name of God sometimes comes up—but he's so not praying.

Dad jumps out of the car and runs into the house. When he doesn't come back, we all follow him inside.

He looms in the doorway. "I called BHPD about what happened. They're looking into it—they said the bus crashed some other properties as well. The private security force is on the way over now." Wealthy neighborhoods sometimes contract out to security

24

companies for additional coverage. When Eva's agent was scouting places for us to rent, this extra security helped sell Mom on our neighborhood.

Not long after, the black and orange patrol car of Sunset Security arrives. Mom leads the officers into our family room. The older officer has a salt-and-pepper crew cut and piercing black eyes. His partner has a round babyish face and thinning blond hair.

We explain how Eva and I first spotted the bus Thursday evening, and how it almost rolled over us today.

"Any other details?" Crew Cut gives me a searching look. This guy must be good at what he does because I'm tempted to confess to borrowing E's new Nikes without her permission, and to eating the last churro when I knew Dad was saving it for lunch. But that's all—otherwise my rap sheet is clean. For a change. "Well, thank you for your help. This bus has been bothering other prominent families in the neighborhood, and we're going to catch them. Fast."

Crew Cut is closing his notebook when Babyface says, "I'd like you to look at this." He holds up a thin black folder.

Dad's face is eager. "You caught them on tape?"

The officer looks puzzled. "What? Oh, yeah, every house has a security camera on the road, so we have lots of shots of the bus. But the license plate is covered with mud—no help there. This is what I want to show you." He darts a glance at Eva, then pulls out an 8 × 10 glossy photo. "It's my head shot. I'm really an actor. The security thing is something I do on the side."

Dad stares at him, fists clenched, like he's thinking about a more hands-on definition of the words "head shot."

The photo slides quietly back across the table.

Crew Cut turns bright red and pulls his partner from the table. "We're on this, Mr. Ortiz." He nods toward the rest of us. "Ladies."

The security team leaves quickly. Dad shuts the door behind them and announces: "Don't worry, Eva. I have a plan."

And as much as Mom has been upset by the intrusion of the Golden Tours bus, it's Dad's words that have her looking worried. Very worried.

"Come on, *familia*. Back to the car. If we hurry, we can pick up Abuela for the next Mass." Mom doesn't mess around with *her* plans. She goes straight to the Top.

She's asking for divine intervention.

*W*e were a regular family living in Anaheim—then my sister jumped into the fame game. Now we have tourists storming our driveway.

A great guy who I liked almost liked me back. But he hasn't called me lately.

A not-so-great guy who claimed to love Lavender is now pranking her with an angry song.

I always want to help Eva, but the bad-luck balloon that's tied to my life sometimes makes things worse.

What I'm saying is: life can have its share of continuity problems. You can think of your own, can't you?

On-screen, though, there aren't supposed to be problems like that. A script supervisor works to make sure that when a character injures his right arm, his sling doesn't show up later on his left. Or that someone who was killed off in scene one isn't wandering around in scene seven.

But sometimes the supervisors goof.

Usually it's small stuff.

Like in *High School Musical,* when Troy tries to ditch Chad to go to the musical audition, he's wearing a belt and white tennis shoes. Then when he makes it to the audition, he's wearing blue tennis shoes and no belt. Or in *Mean Girls,* when Cady walks into her friend's house, Damian gets scared and tosses all the popcorn out of his bowl. In the next shot of Damian, his bowl is full again.

Sometimes the mistakes are more distracting, like a car driving through the background of a shot in *Lord of the Rings,* or a bored grip with modern clothes and a cowboy hat slipping into a scene with Captain Jack in *Pirates of the Caribbean.*

Anyway, with the upheaval of the "Purple Heartache" prank, a continuity error happened. Eva accidentally moved to the wrong side of the couch to deliver a few of her lines. The crew is setting up for a quick reshoot.

Eva and I sit on the set couch, and I help find her spot in the script. Then the stylists bustle me to the side to give E a last look-over.

I have a moment to wonder about Dad's plan to protect us from Golden Tours. Normally, I can't resist jumping in to help—you see, when a librarian and a mechanic marry, they have a good chance of having a child who not only has to *know* everything, but has to *fix* everything as well!

In this case, though, I'll bet the BHPD or Sunset Security will have everything wrapped up fast. Beverly Hills is less than six square miles in size, and the cruisers can get to any part of it in a minute or less. What chance do these extreme tourists have?

I doodle some thoughts, wishing the mystery of why Jeremy Jones has been avoiding me could be solved as easily.

Finally, hair, makeup, and wardrobe meet the script supervisor's approval.

I give E back her script and head to the theater seats to watch her perform.

Roman directs the action. "Okay, Eva. The writers penciled in a few revisions. Read through the lines once, and we'll get it on film right after."

My sister picks up her script.

And my bad-luck balloon goes . . . P-O-P! Again.

There are some constants I don't want in my life.

"New lines? Okay, let's try it." Eva reads out in her strong, clear voice:

> "Caring and smart
> Describe the guy—

There's nothing
He can't learn/won't try.

Though he's a star
On your TV screen
It's never swelled
His ego/turned him mean.

Plus his good looks
Don't disappoint—
Perhaps not a vital
Moral point."

There is a moment of quiet confusion.

Eva just read my doodling!

My private thoughts!

Maybe no one noticed. Maybe no one figured out what she was reading. . . .

"That doesn't seem—" Eva's eyes rise from the script. Lock with mine. And worst of all, fill with pity.

Why doesn't real life come with reshoots?

Scene 7

I go to hide out—*oops,* I mean work on my summer reading— in Eva's dressing room. I'm almost to her door when I hear a familiar voice behind me: "Hey."

"Hey."

My body bypasses my brain, and a wave of happy rolls through me. I should not be this glad to talk to Jeremy Jones, but I *am* this glad.

"How are you, Jessica?"

I'm short, dark-haired, and sane, Jeremy, but these days I guess you go for tall, blond, and reality-challenged. I steal a closer look at him: same blue-eyed, *Tiger Beat* Hot List guy as ever. There are no outward signs of the stress that constant Paige exposure must wreak. "Fine."

"Are you . . . doing that thing you do?"

Flying my bad-luck balloon?

Angering the producer with misread lines?

Wondering what Jeremy is talking about?

The guy is going to have to get a lot more specific about which thing I do.

"How you investigate things? Like the Murphy prank?" Jeremy was a great partner early in the summer when we caught a lighting tech who was stealing from the show, but there's not much of a mystery here now.

"We already know who did it. What's to—" I catch sight of someone over Jeremy's shoulder. "Uh-oh. Hide me."

"What? Is it Murphy? Is he here?"

"No, not him." Okay, when I mentioned that Roman Capo was the *Two Sisters* producer, I forgot to mention his other identity: Jessica Ortiz archenemy. My bad luck has caused such trouble on his sets that today's script screwup doesn't make his top-ten list.

Jeremy looks over his shoulder. "I think Roman is waving to you, Jess."

"No, he's not." I try to hide behind Jeremy. "He can't stand me."

"He's got a big smile—"

"Have you forgotten? I'm a natural detective. I know things about people." I make the mistake of peeking over Jeremy's shoulder. My eyes catch Roman's. I'm not turned to stone, but that would probably be a better fate than the usual reaming he gives me.

Jeremy takes my elbow protectively. So he's dragged along when Roman throws out an arm—he wouldn't swing at me, would he? *Would he?*—and tries for a one-armed hug. "Babe! There you are, sweetheart."

I've ducked out of Roman's arm path, so he winds up whapping Jeremy on the back. Roman gives me a huge grin. "Good to see you, kid."

I respond. "Dabba dabba dabba duh?"

Did he pop a contact lens and mistake me for Eva? I am wearing some of her things . . . her shirt, pants, shoes, socks, bracelet, earrings, nail polish.

Jeremy whispers, "Killing you with kindness, huh?"

"Jessica! You always keep it lively!" Roman turns to Jeremy. "Jeremy, the director wants to show you the ladders for that giraffe rescue scene."

"The 'Necks Chance' episode? But that's not for another month."

"And yet you're leaving. Now."

Roman bares his teeth at me—um, I mean he smiles—and drags Jeremy away.

Whoa. There are some people who make friendly feel so wrong. Roman Capo? He's definitely in the freaky-friendly camp.

I duck into E's dressing room. Keiko is reading through scripts. "Keiko, does Roman like me all of a sudden?"

"Unlikely."

"But he—"

"I heard it all." Keiko frowns. "Look, Jessica, when it seemed like Jeremy and Paige started dating . . . they got a lot more coverage. The show got more publicity. There will be pressure."

Pressure? "Roman swooped over to keep me away from Jeremy? That's . . . that's insane."

Keiko shakes her head. "No, babe, that's showbiz."

"Don't worry, Jessica!" Eva rushes through the door behind me with her script still in hand. Could I tear out the page with my poem? E grabs my hand and squeezes. "I'm going to take care of everything!"

Eva's last plan for helping me with my love life involved first setting me up with the studio owner's egomaniac son, and when that didn't work out (his kiss was worse than his personality!) she created an imaginary boyfriend for me. She named him Obviously Made-Up Guy.

Actually, she named him Heathcliff. But, c'mon, it's almost the same.

"Don't worry about a thing!" She flashes her famous smile at me.

It's a great smile.

I'd smile back if I didn't know better.

A lot better.

Act
II

Living in L.A., everyone likes to mold you and change you. I don't care about fame. I don't care about being a celebrity. I know that's part of the job, but I don't feed into anyone's idea of who I should be.

—JESSICA ALBA

This morning, the studio sends a white limousine. As white as Keiko's hair. As white as her face.

Mom steps into the car. "Keiko, what is it? What's happened?"

Has some prank against Lavender gone seriously wrong? My guess about Murphy is that he won't stop with one practical joke. ("Practical" being code for "not funny.")

Keiko reaches out to touch the back of Eva's hand, lightly.

Uh-oh!

Keiko does not touch, and is not touched—to even shake her hand you have to push through an invisible wall. She holds a *Two Sisters* script in her lap. "Eva, do you remember the five signs of the End we talked about?"'

The End? Keiko never speaks in capital letters!

Eva's face pales. "Death, Love, Specials, Dreams, Dancing."

Keiko hands over the script to Eva. "They've added a dance scene."

"You mean to this week's episode?" Mom looks puzzled. "What's wrong with dancing? Eva is a wonderful dancer."

"Mrs. Ortiz—you should know . . . a dance sequence can be a sign that a show has jumped the shark."

The phrase "jump the shark" refers to a scene in *Happy Days* when Fonzie slaps on water skis and literally jumps over a shark. Jump-the-shark moments mean the show has told all its best stories and desperate days are ahead.

JUMP-THE-SHARK MOMENTS:

- ⭐ **A character is killed (or, *much worse,* brought back to life)**
- ⭐ **The main guy and girl get together**
- ⭐ **Any "very special episode" (issues like drunk driving/eating disorders/getting tattoos in a language you don't speak)**
- ⭐ **Any kind of dream sequence**
- ⭐ **Any kind of singing or dancing "spectacular"**

"But dancing could be good—could be fresh," insists Mom. "Eva's taken professional lessons, and, thanks to her dad, she can really 'drive the truck' and 'spin the pizza.'"

Keiko frowns. "It could be fine. But I have to tell you, in most cases, jumping the shark is followed by circling the drain."

Yikes! The final painful death throes of a series. The writers spew scenes of random romance or danger, crying out, "Look at me! Over here! You used to like me!"

You've seen people jump the shark in their real lives too. Like the guy who buys his hopeless crush an awkwardly expensive Valentine's Day present. (Which sadly becomes circling the drain when he leaves fifty messages on her answering machine to explain about the present. Yes, E's answering machine is mighty full on February 14.)

"But the show is a breakout hit. . . ."

"That was before that *Snake Bait* reality show came on in the same time slot. Our ratings are falling fast, and the show is under a lot of pressure. Now everyone is worried about being a one-season wonder."

Eva frowns. "What do we do, Keiko?"

"We pursue other projects. Fire up some publicity—interviews, photo shoots—keep getting you out there." We all take in Keiko's shudder. "The public won't know about the . . . *dancing* for another few weeks."

*D*ancing may be a peril to the show, but it's fun to watch. Lavender, especially, is a stylish dancer with a lot of moves. Is she the *best* dancer up there?

C'mon, friend, there's a Mexican girl onstage!

The crew starts stamping their feet and clapping as classic (and radio-edit clean) Eminem blasts, and the girls fling themselves off the furniture and pound the floor.

The dance is supposed to look spontaneous, but every movement has been planned by a choreographer from the Dance Arts Academy. There are pieces of colored tape on the floor to show where to step. And, most helpfully, there are professional dancers moving in front of the actresses so they can imitate each motion.

The music and action are all fun. Almost as fun as Paige's new hairstyle.

During the days after her "accident," Paige claimed her little dog, Tinkles, was suffering from sympathetic shock. So the studio lawyers made Hair Steve style Paige and her pooch! Not long after, Paige lost Tink at "either LAX or Whole Foods." Which I guess was also a shock to Tink, but I prefer to think he found it a relief. Steve is getting a little revenge with Paige's new look: the frizzfest. She could house a family of birds up there.

I whisper to Steve. "Paige's hair, it's so . . ."

"Afrofabulous, I know. This week's guest star rocks that look, and I couldn't resist seeing Paige in it. After all, I had to give her mutt a full-body shampoo and curl!"

"Guest star . . . ?"

At that moment, Roman stops the rehearsal to make an announcement, revealing the identity of this week's Very Special Guest. She is one of the most talented singer-actress-performers in the world.

Everyone thinks that's good news.

Everyone but me.

Why? Because the greater the talent, the greater the loss if my jinx does turn toxic.

My solution: avoid, avoid, avoid.

I'm going to pretend she doesn't exist. Keep out of her way. Not mention her name. Anything to break the jinx.

This is one time I won't be destiny's child.

I'm in the front row of the theater, sorting a pile of fan mail, when Jeremy drops into the seat next to me.

"Hi."

"Hi."

Then he says other things. Something about Petunia. Something about his brother. Something about this graphic novel he's been reading.

I can't concentrate on his small talk because I can feel what's coming. A question. That I don't know how to answer.

I shuffle through the envelopes. Jeremy reaches over to help me slide in the signed pictures of Eva. If you write to her fan club (ForEva Friends), she'll send you back a picture that says: *Shine on, sister! Love, Eva.*

Jeremy is talking.

I'm thinking.

He's talking.

I'm thinking.

Then he's asking. There's no way to avoid the Question. "When are you bringing Heath by?"

"Who?" How clever, Jessica. Pretend not to know who he's talking about. That should buy you . . . another two seconds!

"Your sister said you were seeing some guy."

My sister made up Heathcliff as my fake boyfriend, and Jeremy believed it. I've been trying to come up with a graceful yet credible exit for Heath. Either joining Pet Rescue in Canada or sending his band on an all-Asia tour—whichever sounded less made-up.

But suddenly those stories sound like something that . . . Paige would say! There's only one exit that makes sense now that I'm face to face with Jeremy: the truth.

I look down, talking to the picture of Eva I'm holding in my hands. *Shine on, Jess.* "There is no Heath. He was made up."

"Made up?"

"Yeah, there's no such person. Embarrassing, huh?"

"No." I sneak a look over at Jeremy. The way he's smiling is making me smile. He whispers next to my ear. "No one needs to know."

"Yeah?"

"Yeah."

And then . . .

My.

Bad.

Luck.

Balloon.

You can almost see the sharp needle headed for the smooth surface, now, can't you?

My sister's voice booms from the stage: "Jessica! Where's your *boyfriend*?"

Instantly, the place seems to fill with people: the camera crew, Lighting Guy Bob and his assistants, Craft Services, Roman—even the makeup, hair, and costume stylists have found an excuse to be on the scene to witness my embarrassment.

I have *never* been this mad at Eva!

My brain is so fogged by betrayal that I can't get my Pet Rescue/rock 'n' roll fib straight. All I choke out is: "Pet . . . tunes."

"Petunes?" Paige repeats, from the stage. Oh yeah, she's arrived too. "Isn't that your little dog?"

If I had a black hole handy, I don't know who I would drop it on first: Eva, Paige, or me.

My sister's smile gets bigger and bigger; she's approaching full wattage. "Oh, Paige, that's funny. Petunia is first in Jessica's heart, but look . . ."

A tall blond guy enters, stage left.

For a moment, I think he's Jeremy—even though he can't be sitting beside me with his jaw hanging in surprise and walking down from the stage at the same time. Maybe *Jeremy* thinks it's Jeremy—the guy looks that much like him.

Or does he?

As he gets closer, I can see that the similarity is a trick of the light—his hair is a white bleached blond with dark roots, the jaw is more square, the eyes are greenish, not blue.

"It's Heathcliff," my sister says triumphantly.

It is?

Scene 3

*M*y sister would do anything for me.

You might think I mean she would go out of her way to help me, and that's true. But what I'm really trying to say is that she would do *anything*—as in, *What has she done this time?*

My sister races down from the stage to push my "boyfriend" toward me. "Say hello, Jess!"

Heathcliff leans toward me, maybe for a kiss or a hug, but I'm so startled that I half stand and we clonk heads.

"How romantic!" Eva says gaily. "I bet . . ."

The world will never know what Eva was about to bet.

I haul her off to her dressing room by the elbow. Heath follows and waits outside.

Eva is bursting with her news. "Jess, you know how I'm sure I should have gotten the Scarlett Johansson role in *Wisconsin Girl*?"

"Yeess." Eva was hopeful that she'd land the part in Sophie Cassala's new film—right up until it went to Miss Scarlett.

"Turns out I'm a natural at casting! It's Peter's first day as an intern, and as soon as I saw him, I knew he'd be perfect for the part."

No.

It can't be.

She wouldn't have . . .

She couldn't have . . .

She did.

"You cast the part of my boyfriend!"

"Yes! Isn't Peter fantastic?

"You cast the part of my boyfriend!"

"He did a great reading with me, and has improv skills that could be useful. . . ."

"You cast the part of my boyfriend!"

"Yeess!" Eva's bubble of happiness lets out a little air. "Don't you like him? The looks are right on the money. It's only a walk-on part right now. . . ."

Sometimes there is no point in talking to an insane person, I mean, an actress, I mean, my sister!

I open the door to my sister's dressing room and let in my new boyfriend. Up close, I can see he's bigger than Jeremy, broader, and plain taking up more room. "Heath . . ." Wait, that's not right. My words can't catch up to my confusion. I try again. "Peter, I'm sure you're great and all, but this is impossible. You're impossible."

"I thought I was imaginary."

"No, you're definitely impossible."

He raises one eyebrow. "Could we settle on really unlikely?"

Oh, boy.

Oh, imaginary, impossible, really, *really* unlikely boy.

Scene 4

In case you're wondering what someone at an ambush lunch with her fake boyfriend at the studio commissary would be thinking about, here it is: *Is this a date? Is this the third boy I've dated? That's kind of a lot—though the Alex Banks date ended in a slobbery kiss, and the Jeremy date was followed by a huge misunderstanding. Is this soggy mac and cheese with a fake date my best date? At least to date . . .*

". . . is this a date?"

"What? No. Date? Huh?"

Peter is picking through his piled-high plate of food. He points to a piece of fruit that is definitely a date. "Then what is it?"

I look him right in the shoulder. "It's a mystery to me."

He goes back to eating. By the way he's digging into his meal, he may not have eaten breakfast this morning.

Or dinner the night before.

We slogged through the food line, and he grabbed two or three of everything. The only thing he passed on was the bill. He jerked his thumb at me. "She's got it."

Date etiquette—apparently not part of the screen test.

Peter is plowing through a second apple pie. He's one of those people who's comfortable with silence.

I'm comfortable too.

Very comfortable.

"What's your last name, Peter?" Okay, I'm not comfortable with *long* silences—more like pauses. If it gets too quiet, I worry a shy spasm will hit me.

"Banks. Peter Banks."

Banks? Where have I heard that name before?

Oh, that's right: every-*freaking*-where!

OMG! Only E would care more about how a guy fits the part than that his family owns the studio. And what is his relation to . . .

Peter drops his voice. "My bro Alex told me you met—and you got really attached to him."

Only by force of lip suction! That I fought with all my strength!

Peter doesn't notice my outrage. "Did Eva give you the story about how you and Heath met?"

"What?"

"It was at a local carnival. I climbed onto the Ferris wheel to ask you out."

I drop my pudding back on my tray, and Peter starts eating it. "That's a total rip-off of *The Notebook*!"

It could be worse: my sister had also been watching *While You Were Sleeping* recently. At least I didn't meet Heath over a comatose body.

"Whose notebook got ripped off?" asks Peter.

"In this movie, *The Notebook,* the hero and heroine—that's how they meet, at a carnival. Peter, we can't—"

"Peter?" Jeremy has appeared at my side. The one time my Jeremy radar would be helpful, it does not buzz a bit! He must be wondering how my fake boyfriend sprang to real life. "I thought it was Heathcliff?"

"That's me. Heath Peters." Peter holds out his hand for a who's-more-manly grip-off. "Peter is a pet name, right, Jessica?"

I can't answer. I've finally congealed into one hundred percent pure embarrassment. My almost-boyfriend and my fake boyfriend stare each other down.

Please . . . please just wake me when the pain stops.

But there is little chance of the pain stopping, because I see something.

A gleam.

In Peter's eye.

He's planning something, and it can only be . . . horrible. "I guess Jess is getting back at me for my nickname for her, right?"

Do I deserve this? Yes, I lied about having a boyfriend, but torture-by-nickname is too cruel a punishment!

Jeremy doesn't want to know. Maybe he'll walk away. Maybe he won't ask. . . .

"Teasy," Peter says. "Short for Ortiz."

The good news? I'm only screaming on the inside.

"Peter, Jeremy knows the truth. Explain that Eva put you up to this."

"Sure, sweetie—"

"I'm not your sweetie!"

"I mean, Teasy."

Grooowl.

Both boys stare.

Whoa! Did that noise come from me?

Cool.

"Okay, okay." Peter holds up his hands, surrender-style. "Peter Banks. I'm interning on the set, and Eva gave me my first assignment."

Jeremy is confused. "Assignment?"

"She said it's kind of a role-playing thing. I guess this immersion acting is the new thing. Blurring the lines of—"

I cut him off. "Thanks, Peter."

He shrugs and rises to leave.

I reach out to take his arm. "And Peter?" I give his bicep a pinch.

"Was that for 'Teasy'?"

Of course it was! I nod.

He grins. "Worth it."

Jeremy stares at me. "Do you ever think your life is getting a little . . . strange?"

I sigh. "Yeah. Continuity. It's a challenge."

Jeremy sits down. Not in Peter's seat across from me, but right beside me. There's a moment when we look at each other.

Happy.

Peaceful.

Brief.

"Jessica Ortiz? Jeremy Jones?" An assistant from the set holds out two purple envelopes. "These are for you."

I tear open my envelope with a feeling of deep—and as it turns out, fairly reasonable—dread. The message:

> Urgent! See me when you get this note!
>
> —Lavender

My moment with Jeremy fades to black. Or at least to a deep, dark purple.

M y feet drag me to Lavender's dressing room. Jeremy is at my side, but this is not how I want to spend my time with him. Especially when I don't know how much time it will be.

I knock on the door.

Lavender flings it open like she has been waiting on the other side. She grabs the note from my fingers, tears it to bits, and grinds the shreds under a lilac heel.

However crazy I go, it's comforting to know that Lavender will always be one level higher on the nutter scale.

"Y'all got them too? Ah didn't send them."

"You didn't?"

"It's some prank of Murphy's. He sent out a bunch of notes, and people have been pounding on mah door all morning." She points to the wads of envelopes in her violet trash can. "It's driving me crazy, but no one is taking me seriously. All Roman can talk about are the falling ratings. And the security guards here—" Lavender looks mad enough to spit.

I know why. Reginald, the head of security? He would never be confused with a klieg light for brightness.

Jeremy looks at me curiously. "What about you, Jess? Are you getting involved? I know you love a mystery."

Mystery? This is hardly one of those thrillers where it's always the least likely suspect: *Wow, the killer was the semicolon on page seventeen? I never saw that coming!*

"We already know who the bad guy is. His song is number one on iTunes this week."

"Whoa. Number one?" Jeremy scratches his head. "In that last line, was the Georgia peach stuffed with flies? Or with goodbyes?"

"Flies. But goodbyes isn't bad either."

"The best kiss-off song is Justin's 'Cry Me a River' for Britney, but this—"

"Do y'all mind?"

Oops. Lavender's doorway—not the ideal place for this discussion.

She shuts the door with a slam.

Jeremy looks at me. "Jess, there *is* a mystery: how is Murphy getting on set?"

*g*eremy and I take a walk. We're headed for Reginald at the check-in desk, talking excitedly. "No one seems to be taking Murphy's pranks seriously."

"Well, it's small stuff. Rigging a stereo. Sending notes."

"Jessica, that's not the reason, and you know it."

He's right. I do know.

The real reason there's no rush to protect Lavender from these dumb jokes? In a word: history.

When Murphy was dating Lavender, he taped an episode of his *Crank Pranksters* show—with the *Two Sisters* cast and crew as the unknowing stars. Lavender claims she didn't know anything about it, but people aren't sure they believe her. Did she help set us all up? Either way, she let Murphy on set, and people aren't racing to protect her from his payback.

We turn out of the dressing room corridor and we see—and hear—someone I'd rather avoid. She's not the Very Special Guest Star, but is she special to Jeremy?

I admit it: the long blond curls, the high, toned cheekbones, the long legs . . . yes, the stunning visuals are there. But the audio portion of the program? Listen in. . . .

Paige squawks into her cell: "I need to have the new Louis Vuitton hobo bag before that Simpson sister. If she beats me to the next It Bag again, I will die. Do you hear me, D-Y-E, die! My life is on the line!"

Or at least her hair color.

Every month a new teen magazine votes her "best lips," but they don't have to hear what comes out of them.

She flicks off her cell and catches sight of me and Jeremy. "There you are, Remy. Roman wants us . . . I mean, it's time for us to have lunch."

At three o'clock?

Jeremy looks at me like there's something he wants to say but can't. "I've got to go . . . to work . . . I mean, to lunch. I've got to go, Jessica." His blue eyes are unhappy and guarded.

Paige spins away with a perfect toss of curls. He follows.

There are millions of guys who'd chew tinfoil if it was served on a date with Paige Carey. But is it possible that Jeremy Jones *isn't* one of them?

*R*eginald's uniform is a plain gray top and pants; his sheriff-style badge says BANKS BROTHERS STUDIOS in gold letters.

He sips his brimming cup of coffee and lets me look at the check-in sheet. No questions asked. "Sure, kid. Anything for Paige's sister."

Are you getting the picture about security on the set?

"I'm Eva's sister, Jessica. But thanks." I look over the sheet. No names jump out at me.

It was a long shot that Murphy was signing in at the front door. And probably too much to hope that his pseudonym would be Lavender's Angry Ex.

"Reginald?

"Yes, Jenny?"

"Jessica. Are you always on duty here? You don't step away?"

"Always here." I stare at his coffee. "Well, I ran to get a cup of java from Craft Services. But I raced back. Only gone a minute."

He pats his face like he worked up a sweat hustling.

But if he was moving so quickly, then how come his cup is full *to the top*? Wouldn't some of the coffee have sloshed out as he ran?

"Reginald, I know the people who work on the set every day don't have to sign in, but does everyone who's not a regular have to?"

"Everyone."

If Murphy hasn't been on set, then *is* it an inside job? Is someone working with him? Who could be that angry with Lavender?

At that moment, Peter Banks walks by. He throws a "Hey, Teasy" my way and looks straight through Reginald like he's invisible.

"Reg, you didn't exactly check *his* ID."

"He's a Banks." Reginald scowls. "His ID says 'Don't bother me, my dad owns the building . . . and your butt.' "

There do seem to be Banks kids around a lot. They start off interning in the writers' room on Monday morning and are producers by Tuesday afternoon.

Natural talent.

At choosing their parents, that is.

I decide to do a little asking around. Has anyone seen Murphy?

I head to the props department first—since the radio sabotage was the first prank—but the manager doesn't answer my questions. She is furiously packing away her treasures. "The Banks family is on their way! And this whole studio is their toy store. Remember when we hosted that party for the new Mrs.? She admired the couch from the Boston Beanery set, and we had to ship it to her house—that night!"

It's true: that week's Beanery scenes had to be filmed in extreme close-up. In case you were wondering why that discussion of hot chocolate versus green tea was so visually intense.

As I head back into the hallway, I should be on my guard. But I'm not.

I spot the crowd of suits and smiles, but it doesn't slow me down. I wish it did.

Then I might have seen him first. And found something clever to say—or to hide behind.

"Hello, Jessica."

"Oh, hey, hello . . ." Mentally calling someone Mr. Squishy Kisser does not help when suddenly faced with the real person. ". . . Alex."

Alex Banks—Eva had set us up on a blind date. If you've never been reminded of an overactive sprinkler system while kissing, then you haven't been kissing him.

Roman and some studio chiefs are giving the Banks family a tour. Every comment that the silver-haired, power-suited Mr. Banks adds looks like gospel to Roman, who grins and nods harder than a jackhammer.

"Friends, Roman, countrymen . . ."

Roman holds his sides with laughter as if he's never heard that one before. "Hilarious!"

Mr. Banks spouts on like a man used to hearing himself speak publicly—and to enjoying the sound. Peter nods at me, but it's Alex who steps away from the group.

Alex is wearing a navy polo with BANKS BROTHERS STUDIOS sewn on in gold. His ring is stamped with a giant *B,* as are his baseball cap and belt buckle.

Oh, yeah, he's that guy.

"Jessica, what a *coincidence* running into you here."

I shrug. Whatevs.

He looks the same: wavy black hair and enormous white teeth— though maybe they look overlarge because he's standing too close. He moves so far into my personal space that I should charge him rent.

"I guess you had *no idea* I'd be here today." He nods at the blue flyers taped to the walls: *Welcome the Banks family! Today at 4 p.m.*

His gray-green eyes look way too intense for our one-date history. Then he grips my arm and breathes into my face. "Look, Jessica. It's over. You have to let me go."

"Huh?" *Dude, you are the one holding on to my arm! Let me go!*

"It's my fault." *Alex is finally talking some sense. . . .* "I'm not an easy guy to forget." *Blathering insaniacs never are.* "I know we had one of those movie moments together." *Was the movie called* The Ego that Ate L.A.*?* "But it's not going to happen for us. So please, stop following me around."

"Let go of my arm, Alex. Now."

Alex slowly unfolds his fingers. "You're a strong girl. You'll get through this."

Yes, but it would help if I had a shovel to get through all the manure you're spreading.

The family has walked on to the next part of the tour. A fierce-looking dark-haired girl comes back. She gestures for Alex. Before he walks off, he whispers: "Sorry, Jess, but there's no one else like me."

Yeah, well, here's hoping.

I rub the sore spot on my arm. "Twerp."

He doesn't hear me, but she does. She turns around, fast. "Do you know who I am?"

"No."

She crosses her arms and gives me the stink eye. "I'm Alex's sister."

What can I say? "Do you know who I am?"

"No."

"Thank goodness."

And I'm out of there.

I hope I never have to deal with that family again—and you can take *that* to the bank!

Scene 7

*E*va is supposed to be relaxing in her dressing room, so I'm holding her ankles while she burns through power sit-ups. "Am I great with the casting, or what?"

"That depends. Do you define 'great' as 'skilled at embarrassing my sister in front of everyone on set'?"

Eva frowns. "Jess, it seemed like people thought Heathcliff was made up or something."

"He *was* made up! By you! And you gave him the most obviously fake name in the universe."

"Real people are named Heathcliff! Like that cat in the comics. And the guy in the *Wuthering Heights* miniseries. Besides, no one had met Peter before—who could know he wasn't really Heath?" My sister has a slippery sense of reality—but you knew that. "Okay, now listen, Jess. You have a big cheerleading competition coming up. . . ."

"What? I do?" I'm fairly dangerous when I'm just walking around; I'm not sure we should add basket tosses and backflips to the equation.

"I'm talking about your breakup with Heath!"

"My *what*?" It's only because I'm a model of restraint and sisterly affection (and I'm ever so slightly scared of the gleam in E's eye) that I say: "Eva, I don't need to break up with my imaginary boyfriend."

"Of course you do! Heath will have much more credibility if you have a breakup scene." She doesn't wait for me to respond. "So you're the leader of this cheerleading squad, and you find out that your team captain has been stealing routines from an inner-city squad. You and your boyfriend break up when . . ."

Yes, my sister stole her breakup plan from the movie *Bring It On*. I'm partly insulted to get served a used breakup plan, but partly flattered to get cast in the Kiki Dunst role.

The crazy is catching around here. Save yourself.

"Jessica, you guys will have to rehearse. Do you think you could cry on cue?"

"I kind of feel like crying right now."

"Great! Hold on to that! You can use it! Now, where's Peter? You'll have to practice together."

My sister went to a lot of work getting me a fake boyfriend, so I don't say, "E, let it go already." She'll come out of dramarama mode, and it will all blow over. Instead I share an emotional truth: "Eva, I love you. When the crazy van comes for you, I'll hide you in my basement."

E grins and pulls herself into a sitting position to throw an arm over my shoulder. "Thanks, babe. Back atcha."

Scene 8

*K*eiko needs help carrying Eva's fan mail out to her assistant. I throw piles of envelopes into a canvas bag, and we head onto the lot, blinking in the late-afternoon sun.

I always like walking across the lot. If the elephant doors (yes, you could fit a you-know-what through them) are open into one of the studios, I might see an alien landscape or a small town from a hundred years ago or a modern (though miniature) city . . . any story could be coming to life. Today the studios are empty, reminding me only of airplane hangars—empty with just the usual mattresses roped to the walls to muffle sound.

"Coming through!" A delivery guy wheels around us on his bicycle. Sound is also the reason that golf carts and bikes are used on set—they're *quiet*. So you don't hear horns blaring or motors roaring in the background of a shoot. (At least you don't until Golden Tours tracks Eva down here!)

Our path takes us away from the studios and through the small "town" that Banks Brothers uses for outdoor scenes. Most of the buildings are facades—if you walk in the front door, you go right out the back. Only, the buildings don't have back doors, they have two front sides—to double for twice as many shoots.

"Keiko, I'm trying to figure out the Murphy pranks. Find out how he's getting on set. Any ideas?"

She shrugs distractedly. Then, instead of answering my question, she says: "You'll stay away from the studio for a while."

"What?" I can't have heard her right. "What'd you say?"

Keiko doesn't look at me. Instead she points to a man climbing a tall tree. "See that worker up there?"

"The gardener? Trimming the tree?"

"He's not trimming it. He's winterizing it." Keiko explains: The guy we're watching is plucking the individual leaves off the tree. The tree is green and full in our late August weather, but *Two Sisters* needs it in an autumn scene. The tree will be stripped, and then have multicolored silk leaves applied for the fall scene; later the silk leaves will be replaced with the water and paper mix that the folks at Snow Business trick viewers into thinking is real snow.

"Wow, that's incredibly . . ." . . . *Irrelevant to you kicking me off the set!* "Um . . . what are you saying?"

"Appearances matter. For the moment that something is caught on film, it's got to look right. Not *be* right—look right." Now she does turn to me. Keiko pours on the sugar-speak for Eva, but she doesn't lack directness with the rest of the world. "They decided to make the dance sequence part of Lavender's dream. Where she gets visited by all the pets she wasn't able to save."

Oh, no! "That sounds like . . ."

"A Very Special Episode. Exactly."

A little dip in the ratings and the show heads straight for the nearest shark to jump? And what, exactly, does that have to do with me?

"Morale is going to be low when the Special news breaks. It's best if Eva—and others—don't have distractions, or even anything that could appear to be a distraction."

Distraction? What's distracting about a girl with a Very Special Guest Star jinx? Who gets a lead actress to spend time auditioning interns for roles as a fake boyfriend? Who also might be a threat to the publicity machine that is the *Jeremy-and-Paige: Are They or Aren't They?* show?

Ah. I do appear a bit distracting if it's put like that.

Keiko takes the bag of fan mail from my shoulder and tosses it over her own. "See you, Jess. But not here."

Her voice isn't mean. Just professional. Honest.

Final.

Scene 9

Dad has picked a great morning to go *un poco loco*. I'm being serious. After watching Keiko and Eva leave for the set, I need a diversion, and the man has delivered. Big-time.

Dad's first plan for taking on the Golden Tours intrusion was reasonable: he asked the landlord if we could put up a gate to protect our privacy. The landlord said his award-winning architect created the drive to flow with the natural surroundings . . . *blah, blah, blah* . . . no. No gate.

Then Dad called upon one of his favorite expressions: "If it's not the transmission gasket, maybe it's the torque converter." Mechanic-talk for "plan B."

B for Bolder. If you're an optimist.

Or B for Bad. If you're Mom.

"Robert, we can't fill our yard with all these wrecks!"

Dad owns his own garage in Anaheim. He's an expert mechanic, so his shop gets sent a lot of the vehicles that no one else will take on. I don't know how many trips Dad made with his tow truck, but our driveway is crammed with crumbling cars.

"There's no way the tour bus can get in now!" he says happily.

Mom frowns but doesn't say anything when Dad nods for me to follow him over to a half-crashed Audi.

"Help me push this closer to the rose garden." I throw a glance back toward Mom. "Don't worry about your mom. She thinks I'm giving you a pep talk for your new school."

"Um . . . are you?"

"What? Why? They're lucky to have you."

I grin. "Thanks, Papi."

"You should check in with your friend from back home. Leo?"

Leo Takashi—my best Anaheim friend, and the best person for jumping on a bike with, hanging out with, or homework help. As far as keeping in touch? He's pretty far from the best at that.

Leo hasn't even called to see how I'm doing about facing a new school on my own.

"Jess, it won't be easy for Leo. Going to school without you."

Whoa. I never thought of it like that. But I'm glad that Dad did. And then it's less talking, more pushing.

*M*om doesn't need to check out the 302 shelves (Social Psychology) to know people. Dad's cars have not been greasing up our lawn for a full two hours before the head of the neighborhood committee presents a formal letter complaining about "the unsightliness of the property . . . we hereby request the immediate and permanent removal of the offending blemishes to the aesthetics of the community."

And PS: Could Dad give her a discount on some lube work for her Porsche?

Dad frowns. "Well, if it's not the torque converter, maybe it's the oil pan."

Oh, dear.

I follow him back into the house. And as angry as he is?
When the phone rings, it all gets worse.

*P*erturbed.

Displeased.

Could have been happier.

These are some descriptions of how I felt the first time I saw my almost-boyfriend Jeremy Jones smooching up his costar Paige. I didn't realize that the kisses were part of a publicity stunt. I didn't understand that there might be repercussions if my sister told Jeremy that I didn't want to hear his explanation, and if she created Heathcliff the fake-but-strangely-Jeremy-believed-it boyfriend.

Repercussion can be another word for *ouch*.

So I was perturbed, displeased, and could have been happier about the whole Jeremy thing. And my family noticed. I'm not mad at Jeremy anymore, but my family is holding on to the feeling. Big-time. At this point, even my five-foot-nothing, ninety-pound *abuela* is prepared to kneecap Jeremy on sight.

Is it wrong that this makes me feel loved?

Anyway, that's why my dad is steaming. He is standing in the kitchen with his thick fingers squeezing the body of the phone. "Jeremy who? *Who* is this? Who *is* this?"

I think the hours Dad spends under the hoods of countless old cars are devoted to thinking up new ways to embarrass me. Either that or he has an astonishing natural ability.

"Dad, *please,* give me the phone."

He looks at me, and he is seriously thinking about not handing it over. I only have a moment to decide between the Big Brown Eyes approach or Angry Teen.

"Please?"

Dad reluctantly hands over the phone—victory: Big Brown Eyes. He sends one last psychic whammy to Jeremy through the line.

"Jeremy?" I hurry outside to the patio for privacy.

"Jessica?"

"Yes?"

"Your dad sounds pretty tired."

"Um . . . he thinks you dumped me, and will pretty much run you over with his tow truck if you cross his path."

"Whoa."

Possibly an overshare.

But Jeremy caught me off guard with this call. Not that I still rely on recovering shy girl tricks like prewriting conversation tips and giving them helpful acronyms likes WAP (Weather, Acting Joke, Petunia).

The pause lengthens.

And lengthens . . .

And . . .

"Smoggy weather, huh?" I babble, pacing around my yard. "Did you hear the joke about . . ."

Jeremy says: "It's okay, Jessica. I think your dad is . . ." Crazy/scary/strange? ". . . great."

Huh?

"You Ortizes look out for each other."

"Great" was not the expected response to "have father, will pound you," but then Jeremy's family sounds completely different from mine. He's never even mentioned his dad.

There's more silence. Then I hear a voice calling for him on his end of the line.

I don't feel the urge to drown the phone in the swimming pool, so it can't be Paige.

"I have to go now, Jess. Is there a way we could talk?" Is it too obvious to point out that phones have been invented? If Jeremy is acting mysterious to pique my interest . . . it's totally working.

I say: "Yes. You can come over."

Scene 11

*J*eremy arrives, dressed in a white T-shirt and brown outdoorsy pants. He walks around the house to find me skimming leaves out of the pool. (My brain was starting to buzz when I was just sitting around waiting for him.)

I had time to think of a fresh and intelligent greeting. But it flies out of my head, and I blurt out: "How was lunch?"

"Hi, Jess. Lunch? PB and J with . . ." He pauses. "Oh. You mean that lunch thing with Paige? That was at the Ivy."

He says "Ivy" like it's code. But my only translation is: superposh restaurant on Robertson Boulevard.

Jeremy eyes me closely. "You can figure this out, Jessica. The Ivy? Where the paps practically have their own table?"

That's true. The paparazzi have the place staked out. Anytime celebs want an extra shot of publicity, they head right for the picket-fenced outdoor seating.

Waitaminute.

"So you're not really dating her? It's all for show?"

"Roman said the ratings have been slipping lately, and the best thing for everyone is if Paige and I seem like we're dating."

"That's too weird. Didn't your mom talk to him?"

"No." Jeremy looks away. "She said it's only a lunch here and there. What's the difference?"

I must be staring, because Jeremy gets defensive. "Look, my mom is right. Ratings mean jobs. When my last show got canceled, everyone was out of work, like that." He snaps his fingers. "If I can help avoid that, I will."

"Are the ratings that bad?"

"Just compared to where they used to be. *Snake Bait* has come on so strong against our summer reruns . . . people are kind of panicking. Roman even signed the cast up with an acting coach."

Pause.

I have one more question about ratings. How does Paige rate with Jeremy? "Is Paige just going along with this? Or do you think she really . . ." I can't find the words. I had thought Paige genuinely liked Jeremy. But she is incredibly fickle. The flavor of the week bores her after an hour.

"She says I can't handle her truth." I don't have a Paige-to-English dictionary handy, but I'm guessing Jeremy didn't appreciate her fake accident—he couldn't handle her lies.

"What do you say, Jessica? Could I help you figure out the Murphy pranking?"

I smile. We do have a great time when we work together. And that's my truth.

I give up pool skimming, and we flop into lounge chairs facing each other.

We go over the two Murphy pranks: the sabotaged radio cranking out "Purple Heartache," and the lavender notes.

Both pranks come down to one thing: access.

Slipping past Reginald doesn't look too challenging—but still, there must be some trick to it. It's too chancy for Murphy to wait around for Reg to take a coffee break, isn't it?

I tell Jeremy he'll have to be my eyes on the set. Keiko is not the boss of me, but I trust her to look out for E's interests. "I won't be coming around for a while. I'm too busy getting ready for school."

I can't read Jeremy's expression—maybe disappointed? He's

never been to a real school—so he believes me when I say it takes a straight week of preparation.

There's a weird silence, which of course triggers my nervous-babble response. "I'm also working on something closer to home." When I saw that Dad was determined to take on Golden Tours, I knew he'd need my help. I'm officially launching Project Tourist Trap.

I tell Jeremy all about it.

He looks thoughtful. "I've heard about a bus in my neighborhood too."

Jeremy lives a few miles away, in Bel-Air—an even more exclusive area than Bev Hills. There are huge iron gates opening into the neighborhood—but it's not like they could lock the tour bus out. If you look closely, you'll see that the gates are too short to shut for real. They're just for show—that's Hollywood, baby.

Bel-Air is home to a lot of big stars—Leo DiCaprio lives next door to Snoop Dogg and across the street from Steve Martin. The neighborhood is more woodsy and private than my part of Beverly Hills. "Aren't all those homes gated up there?"

"Mostly. But the rumor is the bus has been showing up when the gates happen to be open. Hmm. . . . Let me think about what we can do."

Then we're lying on our backs, talking about . . . stupid stuff.

He starts. "Mexican food or Thai?"

"Both."

"Good. I would also have accepted 'all of the above.' "

"What do you miss from your old home?"

I pause. "Biking around. You?"

"My dad." Jeremy moves on. "Name the four things you can't live without?"

Hair goo, churros, my iPod, my one pair of perfectly fitting jeans, sunshine, cherry lip balm. Which I edit down to: "iPod, sunshine, churros, and . . . charity work. And yours?"

Jeremy says: "iPod, running sneakers, Fat Burger, the History Channel."

I wonder what he's edited. Then again, if he's admitting to the History Channel, maybe he's not holding anything back.

"And now the crucial one: Christmas lights . . . colored or white?"

"Colored."

"Not bad, Ortiz."

"I passed with flying *colors*." Ugh. The pun impulse overcomes me sometimes. "So what do I win?"

We're loose and laughing.

Then—*slam*—we're not.

Because in a perfect world, I'd win a perfect kiss.

In my world? We sit up awkwardly. Jeremy turns red under his tan. "I guess that bus could be coming any second, huh?"

"I don't know." Does it matter?

Jeremy checks his watch. "Wow! How'd it get so late? I should get going."

He gets up. Fast.

I guess that's my answer.

Act
III

Going to a party, for me,
is as much a learning experience as, you know,
sitting in a lecture.

—NATALIE PORTMAN

*E*va, Keiko, and I are headed out to a Los Angeles Charities benefit party tonight at the Getty Museum.

I'm in a flowy blue sundress. E is stamping around the kitchen in a red cocktail dress and kitten heels. The dress is simple and knee-length, but so tight she can barely inhale.

"It's too tight," Mom pronounces for the third time. Dad is hidden behind his newspaper.

"My stylist says this is the Look." E's voice sounds breathy—is she trying to be sexy, or just gasping for air?

"Not for my daughter."

E appeals to Dad. Like he'd ever side against Mom. Eva is desperate because her crush, the lead singer for Spilt Sugar, is going to be performing at the benefit.

"Dad? Help?"

Mom laughs. "You're asking your *padre* for fashion advice? He was wearing corduroy high-waters before he knew better."

The newspaper speaks: "You mean before I knew *you, amor.*"

"Exactly."

Eva angrily taps her fingers against her hips. Something in the motion catches Mom's eyes. "I can't believe you're being so—"

Mom puts up her hands. "Okay, okay. Wear it. See what happens."

"Really?" E is suspicious. Mom never backs down without a good reason. And she rarely lets E attend social functions without her. What could she be up to?

"You and your sister have fun." Mom nods at her stack of library journals. "I'll finally have some time to get through my reading."

"Thanks, Mami!" E gives Mom a huge squeeze, and kisses Dad on the top of his head.

I spot the limo out front and signal to E.

Mom hugs me. "Have fun. Watch out for each other."

"I hope you guys won't be too bored." At least Petunia is staying home, so they won't be completely lonely.

The newspaper drops. "Susan, *both* girls are going?"

"Yes." After a moment, Mom's face lights up. "Yes! Both of them!"

"A night to ourselves!"

"Can you believe it?"

There is a sudden . . . and the only word is *joyful* . . . frenzy of laying out the good china, lighting candles, and tossing all my and E's music out of the stereo.

Eva and I slip out the front door. The last thing we hear is the musical stylings of Disco Dan's Groove Hut.

All in all, a narrow escape.

*H*ow do people walk into a room and start talking?

Shyness, for me, has been the creature from the black lagoon—lurking, waiting, ready to attack. I cautiously make my way through social events, all the while hearing the scary *Jaws*-like *dum-dum, dum-dum* theme music playing in my head. Will this be the time that I embarrass myself . . . or, *worse,* Eva . . . beyond redemption?

I'm walking through one of the sculpture galleries. I left E and Keiko by the outdoor stage. E isn't moving—she said she didn't want to miss the arrival of the band, but I suspect she can barely walk. She had to lie flat on her back in the limo, with her legs across my lap, to inhale properly during the drive.

Pathetic? Possibly.

But I have to admit, when she's vertical, the dress does look good on her.

The Getty Museum, all glass and gleam, is perched high on a hill overlooking Los Angeles. The museum is not one big building but a collection of separate galleries set among covered walkways, patios, reflecting pools, and courtyards. The galleries are packed with sculptures, manuscripts, photographs, and paintings.

There are string quartets playing and waiters cruising with hors d'oeuvres. The bits of conversation I overhear don't make me want to join in:

"I eat anything I want."

"I never work out."

"I'm so over the whole nightclub scene."

"Fame is just the price I have to pay for my art."

"I didn't steal him."

I drift along. I don't know much about art, but tonight there are guides offering background on the pieces.

One of the guides catches my eye. "How old are you?" she asks brightly. She's wearing a crimson and black blazer, navy pants, sensible shoes, and a smarty-pants expression.

"Almost fourteen." I bite back a *How old are* you?

"Ah, yes. Powerful, life-changing time. Fraught with inconsistencies: hyperalert to surroundings, or narcissistic and oblivious.

Anxious for knowledge, for *life-to-happen,* but wish to appear cool and detached."

What? Is she talking about me or a work of art? "I don't see any of that in the painting."

"The painting?" She turns to *The Farewell of Telemachus and Eucharis* by Jacques-Louis David. A young woman bows her head against her lover's shoulder while he stares sadly at the viewer. He grasps her leg with one hand and holds his sword with the other. "Telemachus, the son of Odysseus, fell in love with the nymph Eucharis. Tragically, his duty as a son demanded that he leave her to search for his father."

The guide stares like she's expecting me to say something "narcissistic and oblivious": *Whoa, life before text-messaging . . . sounds tough!*

When I'm silent, she raises an eyebrow. "Not that you kids know anything about sacrificing for family these days."

If that was true, I'd ignore Keiko's worries and be on the set of *Two Sisters* tomorrow!

"No need to frown, young lady. Perhaps you like this picture better? *The Drawing Lesson,* by Jan Steen." An artist instructs two students. A plaster cast of a male figure is the object of a drawing lesson, but the studio is filled with other props. "Objects related to the theme of vanity are hidden in the painting. Want to try to find them?"

Look for clues? That I can do.

SOME OF THE PROPS IN THE PAINTING ARE:

⭐ **pens, brushes, charcoal pencils**

⭐ **a skull**

⭐ **a sculpture of an ox**

⭐ **a laurel wreath**

⭐ **a lute**

⭐ **a chest**

⭐ **a carpet**

If vanity is being too proud of your looks, or your abilities, then what would its symbols be? I don't see a mirror—or a personal publicist—so I'm going with my gut when I guess: "The laurel wreath?"

"That's the easy one. Remember, the painting is also about the dark side of vanity."

It doesn't get much darker than . . . "The skull?"

The guide nods. "Ah, yes, life and fame are brief. And what's to show at the end of either? And . . . ?"

"And?" I think of how quickly music fades from the air. "The lute?"

"Yes." She looks almost annoyed that I guessed correctly, and hurries over to a painting of a bullfight.

She's explaining about the artist's use of light, but all I hear is a low voice at my ear: "Teasy, does that dude look like my dad or what?"

I turn. "Peter! I didn't know you were going to be here."

"There are always Banks kids around. I thought everyone knew that."

I look at the bullfighter. "I don't see the resemblance to your dad."

"I meant the bull."

"Oh, yeah. There it is." Scary. The guide has gathered a bit of a crowd, so I whisper to Peter. "Hey, about yesterday?" How do I put this? "Thanks for acting like . . . you know . . . you like me."

"Pretty convincing, huh?" Peter almost smiles. "I do like you, Jessica. Sometimes."

"Like when?"

"I meant hypothetically."

Funny? Not.

"Jess? Anyone else from the show here?"

"My sister and her publicist."

"No Lavender, huh?"

"No, but I'm trying to work out how Murphy has been able to . . ." Peter's attention has already drifted. His interest in the Southern belle is not of the sleuthly sort.

Peter seems interested in the talk about the painting. I'm more of a people watcher.

One guy cutting across the pavilion catches my eye—for an obvious reason. His look inspires me to pull a pen from my bag and scribble a poem on a napkin:

Fashion victim dons
Unfortunate fedora.
What was he thinking?

The guy is wearing a Creamsicle-colored suit and shirt, with a matching hat. Doesn't he know that you have to be in a black-and-white movie to carry off that look?

I'm double-checking the haiku syllable count when the napkin is ripped from my hand.

"What are you writing, Jessica?"

I look up to see that the Unfortunate Fedora was a disguise!

Wasn't I warned?

Didn't Peter just say there are always Banks kids around? Where was the ominous foreshadowing music when I needed it?

"Oh, hi . . ." The pressure to not call him Mr. Squishy Kisser gives me a brain cramp. I blank on his name! His name is . . . ". . . you."

Smooth, Jessica. Very smooth.

"Hi, Jessica." Squishy looks over at his brother. "Hi, Peter." And then this strange energy crackles between them. Like there's about to be a competition.

I make a grab for the napkin, sure that I can pull it away from . . . Alex. That's his name! But he jerks it up in his fist, high over my head. I hate being vertically challenged!

"Please, Alex, give me the napkin. I need it."

A hideous bad-luck streak + writing down my private thoughts = trouble. It's simple math! Why can't I get it!

"You really want it?"

Peter smirks. The gleam is back in his eye. "I *bet* she does."

It's another weird competitive brother moment.

"A bet?"

Now I get what they're competing over . . . me!

"Please, Alex?" I make another leap for the napkin. The one time it would be useful to have Alex crowding me, he jumps away.

"She does want it!" Peter says.

Alex shoves the napkin in his jacket pocket. "Enough to bet for it?"

I shrug. It's hard to take him seriously in that hat.

Alex grabs two more napkins from beside a pile of empty glasses. "Give me the pen."

I take the pen from my bag and hand it over.

He turns his back, scribbles on the napkins, and returns the pen. "On one napkin, I wrote the name of what *you* want. On the other I wrote the name of what *I* want." He puts a napkin in each fist. "Now pick."

"Wh-what do you want?"

Peter makes gross kissy-face noises. To think I actually liked this guy when he wasn't around his brother!

Alex shoots his brother a look and holds out his closed hands to me. "Take your chances and find out."

I reach toward his right hand, but . . . are the corners of his lips tipping up? Is he trying not to smile?

I grab for his left hand instead.

I unfold the napkin and read: "Kiss."

Stupid left hand.

I steal a glance at Alex—and for a weird moment I flash on Murphy. And Golden Tours.

My gut is telling me that he's cheating! That the bet was fixed in some way.

But how?

And what can I do about it?

'Cause I'm not splashing around in his gooey kiss again.

"The girl doesn't like what she read, Lex!" hoots Peter.

Sometimes I wish I had a brother.

Now is not one of those times.

On pure instinct, I tear the napkin into little pieces and throw them onto the tray of a passing waiter.

"You're not weaseling out of the bet, are you?" asks Alex, narrowing his eyes.

"Nope. It said 'napkin.' Hand it over, please."

Peter raises an eyebrow. "Then why'd you tear it up? I don't believe you."

"Oops!" I hope my smile looks convincing. If Alex isn't the cheater I suspect, I'm going to have to take my lips and make a run for it. But then how will I get that poem away from him? "I've got an idea. Show your napkin, Alex. If it has something besides 'napkin' on it, it'll prove mine was the other one."

Alex's face darkens. "Never mind," he mutters. "Forget it."

His brother jumps in to harass him. "Let's see it." He grabs the napkin. Unfolds it. Reads: "kiss." Then he bursts out laughing. "*Bwahaha!* That was a close call, Jessica."

I knew it!

Alex had written "kiss" on *both* napkins!

Alex pulls the haiku napkin from his pocket and thrusts it into my hand. "Keep your love note. C'mon, Peter, Dad sent me to get you. He's in a mood."

The moment of competition is over, and so is the Banks brothers' interest in me. They walk off without a goodbye.

Just for that, I'm keeping the poem.

Scene 3

I push through the crowd back to the stage area. The place is packed with celebs in all phases of their careers.

Keiko breaks down the relationship between fame and time—

and she's way more direct than some symbols hidden in a painting. The three stages of fame:

⭐ **She looks familiar. . . .**
⭐ **Wow! It's her!**
⭐ **Dead or not dead?**

If E had been listening, Keiko would have softened that up, but you see how she talks to me.

Eva is distracted, watching one of the waiters. After a moment, I recognize him. George is the son of one of Mom's Anaheim friends. He and Eva used to audition for commercials together. "George? Is that you?"

He turns around with his tray. "Oh. Hi, Eva." He's too cool. He obviously spotted her earlier.

"Isn't this so funny? Seeing each other here?"

"Yeah, I'm busting a gut." He chews up the word before he spits it out. "Risotto cake?"

"No thanks." There's barely room for a lungful of air inside that dress, let alone a bite of food. "I'm going to study with a new acting coach tomorrow morning. Varjay? Down on Melrose? He works with all the A-listers. Are you still with Mrs. Jameson at the high school?"

"Yes."

"Does she still smell like that?"

"Yes."

"And does the drama room . . ."

"Leak in the winter, boil in the summer? Yes. *Risotto cake?*" This time he's almost threatening her with Parmesan goodness.

"No thanks. But I hope I see you again soon."

George calms down. His hard mask slips a little. "Yeah?"

He's almost smiling back at E, until she adds, "Absolutely. Come back when you've got some pigs in a blanket. Love those."

George spins away so fast that cakes fly off the side of the tray.

"Or spring rolls," E calls after him. "Also good."

The sensitivity chip? Still missing.

"**T**here he is!"

Eva squeezes my arm black-and-blue to alert me to the presence of Spilt Sugar frontman Julian.

One look tells me the guy is bad-boy tabloid bait. The dress code for the party is semiformal, but he takes the stage in a gray hoodie (with hood over head, of course), jeans, black nail polish, and torn-up black Chuck Taylors. He's working that sleepy, unwashed look that I don't really get, but Eva is excited—let's be honest, *too* excited—to see him.

The band launches into its first song. Right away, Julian notices Eva. They've never met, but being a celebrity seems to be like going to a small school—you kind of know everybody else around.

I scan the crowd. I'm relieved to see that the lone Creamsicle-colored fedora is on the opposite side of the dance floor. I can barely make out Alex around the form of his larger friend.

Something about the friend looks familiar—black hair under some kind of wide-brimmed hat, a dragon tattoo climbing the back of his neck.

That tattoo reminds me of . . . Murphy?

Alex could have met Murphy around the set, but are they *friends*?

Before I can position myself for a better look at maybe-Murphy, Julian points at E to join him during the song onstage. Eva is so psyched that she's about to burst.

Then she does.

Burst, that is.

The seams on her dress.

That's right: wardrobe malfunction. The dark side of vanity has a brand-new symbol!

E feels the tear at the same time I spot it. The dress is basically coming apart from the hip up. I throw my arm around her while Keiko moves in from the front.

"We're out of here," Keiko says.

"But, Julian . . ." Eva gestures up at the stage, causing the tear to race up her side.

Keiko is firm. "A world of no, babe." She flips on her cell to call the driver. "Situation Bad Photo. Abort parking. Return to entrance. Repeat: Situation Bad Photo."

Eva is throwing longing looks at the stage as Keiko and I hustle her out of the courtyard. I stick to E's side, my arm around her back.

Weirdly, Keiko has perfect ESP for when a partygoer is secretly aiming a camera phone E's way. At one point, Keiko breaks away from Eva to block a picture that a guy is trying to take with his phone half hidden up his sleeve. How could she have seen that?

Keiko is one eerie addition to Team Eva.

Back home, we exit the limo with Eva looking . . . what's that tabloid expression? "All torn up from the floor"?

Even Keiko couldn't put a smile back on my sister's face—and when her bottomless bag of praise doesn't do it, nothing will. "The mysterious exit, babe! You left Julian wanting more!"

"Yeah. More other girls to dance with," E says miserably.

It does not help that we're hostages. In our own car. In our own yard.

Keiko thinks it's best that we make sure Golden Tours isn't about to unleash a scream team of tourists before we head out. She rushes to the bottom of the driveway to signal that it's okay for us to hustle into the house. I've never heard of a tour bus running at night (brings new meaning to "seeing the stars"), but Keiko is taking no chances.

She waves, and Eva and I make an awkward dash inside—as if cameras might flash at us like lightning.

Mom and Dad are in the kitchen, cooking together. Outside I can see swimsuits drying by the pool. Wine glasses are on the patio table.

"Back so soon?" says Dad. Yeah, they were missing us.

Eva blazes into the kitchen right behind me, holding the sides of her dress together. "I wasn't able to meet Julian! I hope you're happy, Mom!" She stamps up the stairs.

I don't see why Mom is getting the blame, but she's not bothered. She doesn't look up from the dough she's flattening with the rolling pin.

I have to ask: "Mom, how did you know?"

"I've been living with the Gonzalez hips a lot longer than that girl." Now Mom's eyes do rise—straight to mine. "Maybe you'll take more of your *madre*'s advice than your sister?"

I nod. "Absolutely."

Absolutely maybe.

"We're making quesadillas. Want to help?" Back in Anaheim, Mom would have added water to a mix, but tonight they're making the tortilla dough from scratch. Well, technically, they're making it from flour, vegetable shortening, salt, and water.

Dad is wearing his REAL MEN DON'T USE RECIPES apron and a big smile. Eva's tantrum didn't dent the good mood here at all.

"Don't tell Mali!" Mom says happily.

Yes, it is mildly naughty of them to be cooking in our own

kitchen. Our housekeeper, Mali, has ruled the place like it's her private kingdom ever since we moved in.

I help Dad shred the cheese, and it isn't long before I've told them all about our escape from the Getty. Then we're folding the warm tortillas around the steaming cheese.

The delicious smell draws E back downstairs. She's grouchy but not dumb. Fresh Mexican food is the best. And though her bulky white bathrobe is not as fashionable as a little red dress, it does have one big advantage: plenty of room for quesadillas!

Scene 5

*H*ollywood Hype is blaring this headline, but Keiko says not to worry about it because they don't name Eva, and—most importantly—they don't have a picture. Pictures are what people remember.

Unseamly Behavior

What TV teen was near tears
over a tear? While Spilt

Sugar sang, this Latina
lovely split the scene—and
her seams.

Most of the column space is devoted to the fact that Genie
Wolff, the gossip girl who types the Hype, is going to spin off into
her own half-hour TV interview show.

Lights, Camera, Me!

Today I take my talk to
your TV, my dish to your
dial. In addition to this
column, Hollywood Hype will
also air live on E!. Check
your local listings. I look
forward to seeing all the
friends I mention in print,
in person!

I think Genie can count all those friends on no fingers.

The Hype is the most unwelcome news to arrive on our doorstep
this morning . . . but only until a personal courier arrives.

The letter is for me.

The gold and blue stationery, stamped with an elaborate *B*, opens to reveal:

> DEAR JESSICA,
>   YOU WERE BRAVE WHEN WE
> MET ON SET. YOU ALMOST FOOLED
> ME. BUT THEN YOU FOLLOWED ME
> TO THE GETTY MUSEUM. YOU'RE A
> NICE GIRL, BUT YOU HAVE TO
> MOVE ON.
> LOVE (BUT JUST IN A FRIEND
> WAY),
> ALEX

Yikes! If Alex had a side panel of ingredients, it would read: 100% pure ego.

Mom reads over my shoulder. "Ah. I think that boy likes you."

This was the same thing she said when I was seven and Leo would open-mouth chew his food to try to put me off my lunch. Reading Alex's note kind of gives me the same woozy-belly feeling.

Now you know: I don't get *any* of my keen detective skills from Mom.

I head out to the patio. I should hit my summer reading, but I can't stop going over the Murphy pranks and the trouble with the Golden Tours bus.

Weird things feel like clues.

Or if not clues, exactly, then *ways of thinking:* Murphy sneaking to the set—and to the Getty? Peter as my fake boyfriend. Alex always popping up. The Golden Tours bus avoiding the police and the security team. Paige's fake illness.

What's the connection?

I'm feeling drowsy in the great baking sun when . . . Peter Banks appears. Strangely, he's wearing the crimson and black jacket of the guide from the Getty Museum.

"One key unlocks two doors," he says. We're back in the pavilion and he points to a dark wooden mask. "It's a symbol."

"A symbol? Of what?"

Then Peter isn't pointing at the mask. He's wearing it. The mask slips off, and underneath it's . . .

"Jeremy!"

"Huh? What?" I creak my eyes open. Must have drifted off . . . oops, I mean, I must have entered a *Zen meditative state* to reflect on life's mysteries.

Eva is standing over me with the phone. "I've been calling you. Jeremy is on the line."

I take the phone. "Hello? Jeremy?"

"Want to catch the Golden bus?"

"Sure."

"Meet me at the Kodak Theatre. In half an hour. Come alone."

"I'm going with Eva to her acting class. I could see you around four-thirty? Plus my mom has to drive me."

"Okay, okay. Meet me at four-thirty. Have your mom drive you." He pauses. "That doesn't sound nearly as cool."

Sure, rub it in, chauffeur boy. Until something is built within biking distance of my house, Maxima Mom is the only way I can get around.

*E*va is thrilled about the acting class that Roman signed the cast up for. Keiko and I are taking her to her private lesson.

Varjay's program is so popular with big-name celebrities that the paparazzi have the front door staked out.

One guy with a camera longer than my leg thrusts a book at E as she approaches. "Hold the book for a photo!"

The book is yellow, white, and black. The title? *Acting for Dummies.*

He's the one acting like a dummy. Keiko elbows him out of the way.

Eva smiles for the cameras, and we enter . . . a Hallway of Horrors!

Okay, it's just a regular beige-carpet-meets-white-walls kind of place, but some seriously strange noises are coming from behind the doors.

"Elp! Elp!"

"Eek! Eek!"

"Ook! Ook!"

Whistling, chirping, wailing, screaming . . . "Eva, what do they do in this place?"

"Varjay's philosophy is all about throwing off the artifice of acting and getting down to a primal connection with the part."

That explains it. But not very clearly.

Varjay was called to an emergency acting intervention on the set of *Scary Date Movie,* so Eva will be working with Sebastian Curlingham instead.

Before we enter the room, E clutches my arm in excitement. Heat radiates from her grip. "Now, listen to me, promise me, no matter what you say, don't admire Sebastian's accent. In every interview I could Google, he says how flummoxed—or is it gobsmacked?—he gets when people say they like his accent. It's the one comment there is no response to."

"What about 'Thanks, my dad has one just like it'?"

Eva glares at me. She makes the zip-it gesture over her lips. We push into the room. It's empty except for a few chairs and a raised platform with props—a table and a freestanding door in a frame. Light streams in the windows.

If Sebastian was a young American acting coach, he'd be dressed in long denim shorts, sneakers, and a baseball jersey, but he's British, so his blazer and khakis actually fit. He is sharp-eyed under floppy brown hair, and so tall that he stands slouched to one side.

He is still working with Paige when we arrive.

The only other person in the room is a thin blonde in red plastic boots and a microminiskirt. Her face is a color that Mystic Tan would have to call Oops.

Today must be a day when Paige is speaking to her mom. Their relationship swings to extremes. Mama Paige chats on her Razr, scowling at Sebastian.

Sebastian doesn't like Paige's work, but he's so English about it that even his criticisms sound old-fashioned and kind of sweet. "That's not on, Miss Carey."

"Not on" is not a good thing, but it sounds adorable. "Not on what?" I want to ask.

Which would not improve his mood.

"More energy! More energy!"

Paige: tall, golden, gorgeous.

Notice I did not mention "well coordinated."

Sebastian has Paige in such a flurry that she crashes into the door set up on the platform.

C-r-e-a-k!

Over goes Paige. Over goes the door.

I hear Sebastian mutter, "Lovely."

Oh, the Brits. What kind of curse word is "lovely"?

Eva and Keiko help Paige.

Mama Paige hovers around her daughter, wailing. "That hooting and scratching nonsense? So not for you, baby girl! You need to *not think*. And you're great at that. Learned it from me!"

She grabs Paige's arm. They exit, stage right.

I wind up lifting the door with Sebastian.

"On three," he instructs. "One, two, three." We get it up and step back. "That should do it. Thank you."

I find myself caught by his cool gray eyes. "You're welcome. Nice . . ." *Don't say accent! Don't say accent!* ". . . accident."

Oh.

Lovely.

Lovely. Lovely. *Lovely.*

Eva is taking her mark under Sebastian's watchful gaze. Right before she begins, he offers a word of advice. "If you could not do that thing with your breathing—that would be brilliant."

"Breathing?"

"That in-and-out thing . . . never mind."

"What? I want to get this right. What . . . ?"

"No, never mind. Your breathing is fine. For an American. Forget it. Action!"

Eva opens the door on the platform and says: "Hello."

"*Cut!*"

Eva stops. Stares.

"Well done, Eva. Truly. But for the next take, let's make some stronger choices."

"Stronger?"

"More surprising, more extreme."

He wants a stronger, surprising-er, extremer "hello"?

Sebastian has my sister go over her "hello" and each line in the scene again and again. At first, she is filled with her usual ravenous determination, but eventually his critiques have her squirming like an amoeba on a microscope slide. Nothing pleases Sebastian.

A small box shape covered by a cloth sits on a chair next to him. He whips the cloth off to reveal a plastic cage. "Look at him! Look! He is not acting, he just . . . is."

He just is . . . a hamster!

"Look at Twitchers! Twitchers *gets* it!"

The growl in my throat must slip out, because Keiko shoots me a look. "Eva is my sister," I whisper. "*I* can say she's a bad breather, or has a boring hello, but I don't know who *this guy* thinks he is with all his . . ."

". . . coaching?" Keiko speaks in a low voice, but the word stings. Is Sebastian helping Eva in some way I don't understand? *Is* he a genius?

Sebastian sighs. "Eva, could you play it more like a real teen, not so *actressy*?"

Or is he only a genius at freaking out the talent?

I remind myself of my good intention: be here for Eva's support, but otherwise, don't interfere. (Though I almost wouldn't mind if my jinx flared up!)

Sebastian jumps up on the platform to speak privately with E. I don't know what he's saying, but I don't like it. Eva looks shaken. Her fingers tighten on the script.

Sebastian strides off to consult his notes, and Keiko approaches him. "Eva looks a little upset. What's wrong?"

Sebastian sighs. "Wrong with her? Must you ask? She's an *actress*."

Here is where good intentions meet the Ortiz temper.

And where the good intentions get toasted, fried, and served with a slice of angry pie. And believe me, it's the shy ones who have saved up the most sizzle.

I get right in Sebastian's face—okay, technically, I'm about chest-high, but you get the idea. "Look, Captain Oblivious, my sister has more talent than you know what to do with! If you had a single clue about what you wanted from her, she could deliver it wrapped in shiny paper with a bow!"

The room gets real quiet, real quick.

I steal a glance at Eva's face. She's totally white. I've never interfered on set. At least, I haven't interfered *on purpose* before . . . some bad luck with guest stars notwithstanding.

Everyone seems to be holding their breath—except for Keiko, who comes closer to me, edging her shoulder between me and Sebastian—waiting for his reaction.

The reaction?

In a word: unexpected.

"That was entirely . . . what's the word? . . . *real*! Eva—did you catch that? The sparkle! The snap! It was as though this little person—who are you?—was *truly* angry with me. Brilliant!" Eva turns from white to green. "Eva, you must bring *that* kind of energy to the part. Eh, wot?" Sebastian beams a huge loopy smile. "Once more from the top!"

Keiko relaxes her stance at my side, but it's calming to have her near. Especially now. When I realize that I have no idea how to protect E from Sebastian.

Because, that bloke? He's not bowling with a full set of pins.

*E*va heads to the set, and I go home. I know I should dig into my summer reading, but I'm going to have to find out what's so great about Gatsby another time. Project Tourist Trap needs investigating. I'd like to have some ideas before I meet Jeremy at the Kodak.

I decide to start looking for clues by taking Petunia for a walk along the Golden Tours route. There's been no sign of the bus since Dad met with Sunset Security. Have they given up?

I rub Petunia behind the ears and snap the leash onto her collar. I know what you're thinking. The pink and green collar *is* preppy—but my girl has *jowls*. That you could hide apples inside.

She has to get her pretty on somehow, y'know?

I'm partway out the door when Mom says: "Walking Little P? I'd love to join you!"

Suspicious? Very.

I don't need to have logged countless hours watching *CSI* DVDs to know something is up. My mom has some seriously misguided opinions about my dog. She confuses "fuzzy love box" with "leather-bound-book-chewing ravager of destruction." Like it's Petunia's fault she can't read the words *Madame Bovary*.

Mom whispers to me as we head out of the driveway, "Your dad thinks I'm giving you a pep talk about your new school."

"And you're not?"

"Of course not. They're lucky to have you." Mom loops her arm through mine. "You've done such great work on your shyness this summer."

"It's not a crafts project, Mom." Believe me, I'd rather be making photo frames out of Popsicle sticks than dealing with a shy spasm. Clammy skin, trouble talking, face heating up—and no idea when it will strike next. "It's your dad I'm worried about. He's taking this sightseeing intrusion very seriously. I didn't mention it to him, but the bus came by again while he was at the shop."

"When?" How is it that the Beverly Hills Police Department can catch a candy wrapper before it hits the ground, but a screeching gold bus slips right by them? Is it only Hollywood, or is the world full of puzzles?

"Early this morning. You and Eva had left for the acting class." Mom pauses. When she speaks again, I think the sound of construction nearby is drowning her voice, but then I realize that she's almost whispering. "I think I know how they found out our address. I finally got around to sending out change-of-address notes to everyone back in Anaheim."

"But Mom, our friends would never—" Then I remember George the waiter. Not everyone is happy for Eva's success.

My thoughts are interrupted by the *schoop-schoop* of a low-pitched police alarm. The Sunset Security cruiser rolls to a stop beside us.

"Mrs. Ortiz." Crew Cut has rolled down his window to address Mom.

She nods. "Any luck tracking the tour company?"

"Not yet. They're not legitimate, obviously. Not registered anywhere officially. We've heard rumors about an underground tour line starting up, but no details." He frowns. "I got your message that they were on your property again. They bothered some other celebrity families around here too, and then took off for Bel-Air."

Babyface pounds a fist on the dashboard. "It was the worst luck that both the BHPD and Sunset patrols were on the other side of town."

"Maybe they know your schedule?" I suggest.

"Impossible. We make sure we don't have a schedule." Crew Cut's window starts rising. "But don't worry, their luck won't last."

Luck?

Appearing in Beverly Hills at the moment when the BHPD and the security cruisers can't catch them? Hitting the Bel-Air estates at the exact time when gates to celeb homes are open?

I know luck, and the timing of the tours isn't luck.

There's some kind of trick here—something like with Alex and the napkins. This is rigged too, but I don't see how Golden Tours is doing it. Yet.

Mom and I watch Petunia pounce after a bug. Mom asks, "Why aren't you going to the set?"

My eyes slide away from hers. I'm keeping Keiko's request to myself. "I'm getting ready for school. Lots of reading to catch up on."

"Hmm." It's her I'm-not-buying-that-excuse "hmm." She can pack a lot into one syllable.

"Mom, if I told you my staying home was the right thing, would that be enough for you? For now?"

She takes my hand. Squeezes. "Yes, *m'ijita*. Yes, it would."

It's not a mother-daughter moment. It's a person-to-person moment—maybe our first.

Her confidence flows into me.

As we walk home, even the security cameras peering out at us seem to glow golden in the sunlight—but that must just be my mood.

Scene 8

I miss going to the set with Eva. But I try to focus on the one good thing to come out of being banned: avoiding the studio will help me to move beyonc . . . I mean, *beyond* my guest star jinx.

Poolside with the laptop, I'm supposed to be quizzing Eva on the Industrial Revolution for her online class—but it reminds me that in six short days, I'll be going to school. Without her.

So I throw out some questions about her afternoon.

"Jess, you didn't miss anything."

"Really?"

"Really. Nothing." Pause. "Except . . ."

"Except . . . ?"

"There was this chalk outline."

"Yes?"

"Sketched on the floor."

"Yes?"

"In the shape of a body."

"What?"

"Right in front of Lavender's dressing room. Surrounded by yellow caution tape and everything."

"What!"

"But, like I said, it was nothing. Just another prank by Murphy. He made Lavender's dressing room look like a crime scene, including this outline of a dead body." Eva wrinkles her nose. "No one was hurt, but it's *too* creepy."

Girl dumps you, so you write a revenge song, send out annoying notes, and caution-tape her dressing room? I'm filing this under: "Boys—Glad I Never Have to Be One."

"A crime scene? *That's* your idea of not missing anything?"

E shrugs. "And then later . . ."

"There's more?"

"It's not much. I mean, nothing as outrageous as Lavender wearing some color besides . . . you know. It was more that she *upped* the purple."

"Upped?" How is that possible? The girl only wears purple,

plum, grape, violet, and, when she's feeling especially daring, indigo. Her cell ring is "Purple Rain," and I know for a fact that she can't stand Prince.

"This time she was purple *all over*. All over her body. Arms, legs, hands, feet . . . and her face? Well, that was getting more purple by the minute."

"Her whole body?"

"Yep, the whole . . . hmm, not enchilada. What's a purple food? The whole eggplant?"

I sigh. Two pranks in one day? There must be clues there somewhere. Probably sitting right out in the open for Reginald to ignore. "Any leads on how Murphy is getting on the set?"

"No. Security is on it, but somehow that doesn't make me feel real secure." She twirls a strand of hair around a finger. "Like I said, you didn't miss anything."

Obviously my sister and I have different definitions of the word "anything."

E starts clicking on her laptop to replay part of a lecture, and I know I can't put off my apology any longer. "I'm sorry about yelling this morning. In your acting class."

E looks up from the screen. She reaches over to squeeze my arm. "It's okay. I know it was like . . . one of your accidents."

"Hey! I'm not *that* sorry. The guy was a complete—"

Eva holds up her palm. "Sebastian's approach didn't work with me. I was pretty disappointed not to meet Varjay."

"But what's all that 'be the hamster' stuff about?"

E gets her talking-about-my-craft glow. "Acting is all about finding the 'in'—the 'what-it-is' that unlocks the character for you. A way of thinking, a walk, a look—anything that reveals. Different ways of looking at a character, or looking at different kinds of characters—even animals—might open a door."

When it comes to her work, Eva is looking for the crucial clue.

Sometimes we're more alike than I'd guess.

"Yeah, but, E? About Sebastian? You know that he fell out of the crazy tree, right?"

"And hit every branch on the way down." She shrugs. "Sometimes crazy works."

Scene 9

The Kodak Theatre. Once a year, it's the site of the Oscars. On all other days, it's part of a shopping mall. Set designers cover the Virgin Megastore and Sanrio shop, roll away the

Naturally Nails kiosk, and pave the street with a red carpet to create Oscar magic.

"Psst. Jess, over here."

Mom heads to the Virgin store (more Disco Dan?) when I spot Jeremy hiding behind the jewelry-cleaning kiosk. He's wearing cargo shorts and a T-shirt, with his L.A. Kings cap pulled low over his aviators.

Jeremy texted me about the Murphy pranks—he hadn't found out anything new—but he would not reveal why we're meeting at the Kodak. "What's going on?"

"Look at the street."

I look. I see the usual collection of tourists, street vendors, and . . . sightseeing buses. "Lots of tour companies use the Kodak as their drop-off spot." Jeremy smiles. "I thought we'd keep our eyes open."

A stakeout is a good plan.

I could do it.

You could do it.

An internationally recognized TV star who's appeared in countless commercials, soap operas, series, and movies of the week? Not such a good fit.

It's when Jeremy smiles at me that people first notice him.

Conversations are whispered. Heads turn. Then a little girl approaches, and when Jeremy kneels to talk to her, others feel like they can approach as well.

People hover for autographs, talking about Jeremy's different roles. On request, he signs his name and his old tagline: "That's just the crazy talking!" (A holdover from *Sweetness and Sam*—his previous show—that he has *not* been able to shake.)

One mother pushes her little boy forward. "We *loved* you as Little Ricky in *The Last Goodbye II*."

"Thank you."

"Could you say the closing lines? Please?"

"Well, it was a long time ago. . . ."

"Please!" She gives the boy a shove. He looks three years old, wide-eyed, and completely unclear on who Jeremy is. "It's Logan's favorite!"

Jeremy seems undecided for a moment, but then his face changes. He's instantly younger, vulnerable, and pained. "Paw, please don't take Maw and go. Don't leave us. Don't say the last goodbye—again!"

Then the whole crowd shouts: "Nooo!"

And little Logan bursts out bawling—big, sloppy sobs.

What was his mother thinking?

Even grown-ups are sniffling. It's sad the way some people can't separate reality from acting.

Jeremy puts his arm around me, turning us away from the crowd. "Jessica? Are you crying?"

"Wh-what? No, some dirt got in my eye. Ow. It hurts."

We walk out onto Hollywood Boulevard, where another group immediately notices Jeremy. *"Mira, Mami! Es Rico del Pasado adiós dos!"*

I have one word for Jeremy: *vámonos.*

Scene 10

*J*eremy has a new idea. And a new destination for us, walking distance from the Kodak. I tell Mom I'll text her when I need a ride, and a few blocks later I'm facing this sign outside a small stucco building:

MOVIE MAKEUP:
THE FACES FROM OUTER SPACES!

"Interesting tagline, Jeremy. Very reassuring."

He grins. "Not everyone is a poet like you, Jess."

At the front desk, a guy with short dreads, rimless eyeglasses, and a KEEP L.A. WEIRD T-shirt approaches. "Jeremy! I didn't think we'd see you back here so soon."

What? Does Jeremy hang out here? It's not like *Two Sisters* is planning a Very Special Aliens episode. I hope.

Jeremy introduces me to Marcus, who runs the place. "We add the effects that help bring a story to life. But whether it's makeup or prosthetics—it's all about letting the performance come through."

"Prosthetics?"

Marcus explains: plaster casts of the actor's face or body are taken. The cast is the basis for the foam latex that will be applied to create almost any three-dimensional effect. "We make everything from alien faces to full-figure casts."

"Whoa." Forget foundation and powder—this makeover is a *fake*over.

"Yeah. It can get interesting. Especially if we forget to leave breathing holes for the nose! Ha!" Marcus pulls out a binder of costume designs. He flips to a series of drawings showing a blue-eyed blond guy wearing some kind of spaceman costume. "The process starts with the designer's sketch. Let me show you."

I smile. "Hey, this guy looks like you, Jeremy—with a bad case of bedhead."

Jeremy pushes me past the drawing.

Did I say something wrong? "Um, not that I've seen you with bedhead. Or imagined you waking up. Sleep-rumpled. Just a guess."

Sleep-rumpled? Sleep-*rumpled*? Where did that come from? I catch another glimpse of Marcus's T-shirt. I am so doing my part to keep L.A. weird.

"Never mind that stuff, Marcus," Jeremy says quickly. "We were wondering if you could hook us up with some special-effects makeup?"

What? We were?

Jeremy whispers, "Jess, it's the only way for me to be at the Kodak without getting mobbed."

"You mean like a disguise?" I flash on my weird dream about masks and mysteries. Was Eva right when she said, "Sometimes crazy works"?

Marcus nods. "There's no staff here to help, but I could do something quick."

He leads us to a mirrored room packed with makeup kits, wigs, beards, and costumes. There's also a stomach-churning display of warts, boils, and flesh wounds.

"We only use human hair for our wigs," Marcus says proudly.

Yikes! I must touch my hair nervously because he assures me they only take hair from willing (and paid) volunteers.

Jeremy asks, "Marcus, what's the *best* way to disguise someone?"

Marcus grins. "Guess."

I look around the room. Wigs. Beards. Fake noses. Makeup. Hats. Clothes. What could it be?

"Beard?" guesses Jeremy. "Prosthetics?"

Marcus shakes his head. "Expectation."

"What?"

"The best way to fool the eye is to fool the brain first. Say you want to convince people that the new neighbors on your show are from outer space. To establish that expectation, you talk about how strange the neighbors are, their weird habits, the odd lights flashing at their house. By the time you introduce the neighbors, a simple pointed ear has the audience seeing aliens. If the audience *isn't* expecting aliens, then you might need full-body paint and a UFO landing to get your point across."

I think of the *Two Sisters* set. One of the reasons the view of

Boston Harbor looks like water instead of a digital photograph is because the viewer *expects* to see water.

"You guys look around. I'm going to get some other props. I only have time to really do one of your faces, so let me know your ideas."

Marcus leaves. The door closes. Jeremy and I are alone.

"Obviously, you should get the treatment, Jeremy. No one knows who I am."

"No, no. I want you to have fun. I can get a hood or something."

A *hood*? Throw in black sunglasses and you have the guy "celebrity-among-us" uniform.

We poke around the room. I'm playing with a long red wig, but mainly I'm feeling the room get small and the silence get thick.

The questions I can usually keep from buzzing around my brain start barreling in: why is Jeremy helping me with Project Tourist Trap?

Because he likes solving mysteries?

Because he likes *me*?

I thought he did, but he hasn't done anything about it. I want to ask him, but I can never get the words out. This shy girl hasn't recovered *that* much.

But maybe . . . there's something I could do without saying any words at all?

Some Taco Bell napkins on the counter give me an idea. "To decide who gets the disguise, we could each write down what we want on a napkin. Then pick the winning napkin."

Jeremy shrugs. "Sounds good."

"What we really want. Here in this room. Now." I'm staring hard at Jeremy. Is he getting the message? *The possibilities?* "You know? *Really?*"

A knowing light gleams in his eye. We smile matching too-wide grins at each other.

"Sure, Jess."

I take my napkin. I scribble the word: KISS.

Is he writing the same thing on his?

He peeks over at me and grins.

Then I take both folded napkins. I toss them into a cardboard box full of hats.

Jeremy closes his eyes. Picks one.

He opens the napkin. A warm, special smile lights his face. . . .

"Mustache!" he says happily. "I win. What'd yours say?"

"The same thing."

"What?"

"Yep. Same as you."

"Really? You want a *mustache* for your disguise?" He gives me an odd look.

As far as you'll ever know, Jeremy, the napkin says mustache. I reach into the box and tear the evidence to shreds.

What was I thinking, copying Alex Banks? This is one disaster I deserve.

At that moment, Marcus returns, and Jeremy explains how he won the mustache treatment.

Marcus takes a look at me and knows something is wrong. Very wrong. I swing my hair farther over my face.

"Aw, honey, those are the *saddest* brown eyes I've ever seen!" Marcus squeezes my shoulder. Uh-oh! The power of Big Brown Eyes is working against me! "Don't worry, Jessica. I'll make time for *two* mustaches."

"What? No, please, I don't need a disguise. And I really don't want . . . I mean . . ."

"I won't have time to fit you with a matching wig, but I have a perfect plan for that girly hair of yours."

Marcus reaches into the props trunk and pulls out a . . .

Oh!

No!

In this case, "perfect" translates into "Why me?"

*J*eremy and I are back at the Naturally Nails kiosk at the Kodak Theatre.

"Great disguise, huh?" Jeremy twirls an end of his long blond mustache. "It's so . . . what's the word?"

"Itchy?"

"No." He laughs. "Freeing. Liberating?"

My Nose Neighbor? Freeing?

"More like awkward. Or—*achoo!*—ticklish."

"I understand. You get to be Jessica Ortiz every day. Who'd want to give that up?" And this time Jeremy isn't laughing. Just smiling. "That's a great hat Marcus gave you. What kind is it again?"

"A fedora." A deeply unfortunate fedora. Slightly lumpy because my hair is pinned up inside it. No one looks good in these outside a black-and-white movie: it's a fashion rule, and I am *not* the exception to it.

Of course, it doesn't help that I'm also wearing a wide brown mustache spirit-gummed to my upper lip, oversized round glasses, and a baggy green sweater. With a choice of wigs, tiaras, boas, crowns, and cloaks, I had a chance for Jeremy to see me in a new way, and I go for . . . *The Simpsons'* Ned Flanders.

Swell-diddly-*d'oh!*

I notice that Jeremy's attention keeps being drawn to the sidewalk magazine kiosk.

He's looking at . . . I can't believe it!

Tabloids!

E has Keiko deliver every celebrity magazine to our door, but I never thought Jeremy cared about that stuff. . . .

He must catch me staring because he shifts his feet uncomfortably. "It's like hearing people talk about you behind your back. Hard to ignore." He changes the subject, fast. "Do you think the bus will be here on the hour? The half hour?"

I shrug. "There's been no one time that the bus shows up. It seems to be whenever it would be hardest for anyone to catch them."

Jeremy looks thoughtful. "Sounds like they have inside information."

"I thought about that, but the BHPD has a great reputation—and the tour company would have to have people in the police department and at Sunset Security. How likely is that?"

"It can't be a coincidence that they've been slipping through all this time."

That's the same thing I thought—about Golden Tours and my neighborhood. And about Murphy and the *Two Sisters* set. It's so frustrating to know there is a trick happening in front of my eyes but not be able to see it.

We watch the legitimate sightseeing buses fill up and drive off. Yes, this does seem to be the go-to spot for tours. Jeremy whistles happily at my side. I'd like to think it's my company making him so cheery, but I have a bad feeling it's that mustache of his.

Suddenly, my clue-catching is interrupted by a sharp burst of pain. To my ears.

That's right: I hear my sister's voice.

"Jessica! There you are!" Eva is waving at me from across the courtyard. She rushes over. "I'm here for the stakeout!"

She's wearing a black baseball cap, matching T-shirt, skinny jeans, and giant bug sunglasses while clutching a huge over-priced handbag and chatting on her Razr. Why doesn't she just carry a flashing sign that says ACTRESS INCOGNITO on it? "I've got to go, Keiko. Jessica needs me."

Yes, I need her.

To leave the scene! Immediately, if not sooner!

E pets my hat, then claps. "I want a disguise too!" She looks at me more closely. "Only not a really ugly one."

Not. Helping.

"Eva, could you *please* . . ."

Too late. The crowd is upon us.

"Miss Ortiz? I love you on *Two Sisters*! Your tears for poor Calamity Kitty . . ."

"The way you cried over old Mr. Oops . . ." Several people tear up. "The Big Gravity Lesson" was an emotional episode.

Jeremy is backing away, tense and worried. He'll look extremely silly if someone figures out who he is. And with E here, people might *expect* another *Two Sisters* star to be around.

I make a call on my cell. "Situation Bad Photo. I repeat, Situation Bad Photo. Abort stakeout."

"What?" Mom's voice is crackling on the line. "Jessica, talk sense. What do you need?"

*A*s much as I trash-talk the Maxima, I'm always glad to see it drive to my rescue. Not glad enough to let Mom off the hook, of course.

"Mom, how could you tell Eva what Jeremy and I were doing? And drive her over?"

"I was completely helping you, Jess." Riding shotgun, Eva is trying on the hat from my abandoned disguise. Can you believe it? The fedora looks entirely adorable on her!

"I'm sorry, *m'ija*. When you said you were going to the costume shop, I assumed you kids were working on an acting project. You should have told me it was a date."

"Date? Who said anything—"

I stop talking.

There is no subject that further discussion with my mother cannot make exponentially more embarrassing.

It took me almost fourteen years, but at least I've figured *that* out.

We drive to Bel-Air to drop off Jeremy. It's my first glance at his house, or should I say, his *castle*. There are actual turrets that you can see all the way up the winding drive. The white stone building spreads its wings among manicured gardens, with a tennis court and pool visible around the back.

The seats on the Maxima have never felt quite so *vinyl* before.

When we move along the circle drive toward the front door, a Brazilian butler steps out to greet us—apparently English butlers are a bit overdone. Maybe when you have a six-foot crystal fountain in your courtyard that plays "Memories" while the jets spray, you have to worry about which butler is going to put you over the top.

"Bye, Jess," Jeremy says, leaning toward me in the backseat. My sister and mom don't even pretend not to be listening in. E actually drops her Razr when Jeremy speaks close to my ear. His low voice against my hair feels shivery nice. Until I make out what he's saying. "You still have some mustache stuck to your lip."

A Hollywood ending?

Not. Even. Close.

The Maxima is climbing our street when a familiar bus roars up behind us. The speaker blares: "If we climb high enough, we can catch a glimpse of the Pink Palace itself: the Beverly Hills Hotel. The inspiration for the song "Hotel California," and the site of four of Elizabeth Taylor's eight marriages—do you think she got a group rate?"

"Mom! Behind us! It's Golden Tours!"

"Call Sunset!" Mom says.

We're pulling into our driveway when the car makes a funny sound.

Pop!

Pop!

Pop!

Pop!

Mom jerks the steering wheel and stops the car.

"Is something wrong with the car?" asks Eva.

"Nothing's ever wrong with this car, E. You know that." We're blocking the entrance to our property, so the bus drives on.

"Mom, let's go! We can follow them!"

"No, we can't."

"C'mon, Mom, try to see where they're going. Give the police a chance to catch up."

"I mean, we *can't*. Our tires are flat."

"What? *All* of them?"

"Yes, I think there were tacks, or some kind of nails, in the driveway."

"What? It's not enough to barge onto our property—now they're sabotaging our car?" No one hates on the Maxima more than I do, but this is too much!

Mom sighs. Rests her head on the steering wheel. "It wasn't the tour company. Think closer to home."

"Hola, mi amor." Dad's face is at the driver's-side window, looking sheepish.

Oh, I get it.

His plan to at*tack* the Golden bus would have been more successful if he'd let Mom know about it first. Then the tourists would be trapped instead of us.

"Um . . . Susan, I was planning to replace the tires anyway." Dad can't quite meet Mom's eyes as a blush heats the back of his neck.

Ay, Papi! I thought *I* was the worst actor in the family!

Mom lowers her head till it's leaning full on the horn.

Under the noise, E whispers back to me, "Who has weird parents?"

"You do," I tell her.

"You too." It's our old joke.

And it's still true. Completely.

Act
IV

Everyone in high school is in such a rush to date. I think
it's always better to give a relationship time to develop into a
friendship first. . . . I think the real key is patience.

—MISCHA BARTON

I knew Keiko wanted more publicity for Eva, but I never
thought she'd go this far. "Keiko! How could you?"

"It's the hot new show. Eva is lucky to be on it."

"But you're throwing her to the Wolff!"

Genie Wolff, that is.

Keiko, Mom, E, and I are gathered with Paige and her agent in
the greenroom, waiting for the cast of *Two Sisters* to debut on
Hollywood Hype TV.

The greenroom is the waiting area for a TV show. It's packed
with eats, but no one touches them. You don't want to go out with
veggie dip stuck in your teeth or soda splashed on your shirt.

There are TVs in the room, tuned to the show so that the actors
know when to go on. Genie's blue eyes flare from the screen.
She's sporting puffy red lips and a look-at-me dye job, her black
hair streaked with electric green.

I lower my voice so that Eva can't hear me. "Genie is the queen
of mean in her columns. She's going to tear into E!"

Keiko doesn't look up from her BlackBerry. "Genie *is* difficult—
the woman has more issues than *National Geographic*. But you

don't prepare for a show by studying how the host *is*. You study the tapes. How the host handles guests on air. What she wants the people at home to think of her."

That makes no sense.

Until I think of the girl at school who was always rude on the bus and the playground and the bathroom. But get a teacher around? She turned so sweet, my teeth ached when I listened to her.

I watch Genie on TV, and it's the same effect. Under the camera's eye, she's completely friendly. She's tossing valentines at her guests like she's found her inner Oprah.

Moving around the room, I notice one of the Hype interns. He's asking Paige and E if he can bring them anything, but they're so focused on watching the TV, they barely see him.

The intern is soap opera handsome with big white teeth and blue eyes. He looks like the original Ken doll, before Barbie dumped him. Now he approaches me. "Hi, I'm Jed."

And just like that: shy spasm.

I think I say my name. I know I put my cold, clammy hand in his.

There is a theory (in one of the *Why So Shy?* books that Mom got me) that shyness is a defensive reaction to being singled out of the herd. Special attention in the wild can be dangerous—triggering a fight-or-flight response. Obviously, Sebastian brought out the fight. And Jed is bringing out the flight: every thought flies out of my head.

I can hear the blood pounding in my ears: *whoosh, whoosh.* My body temperature swings between sweat and cold sweat.

"You must be Eva's sister, huh? You look alike." He beams an enormous smile down at me. "I bet a lot of people just want to talk to her, but I'm interested in you."

"Oh." My brain races for something to say, or some way to escape.

He grins. "So what do you think of Eva?"

Then I notice that Jed keeps looking over my shoulder at E. I have a sixth sense for when a guy is more concerned about E than me. (Actually, since she's a famous TV star and I'm not, it's really just common sense.)

I'm still fighting the shyness, but I get myself together enough to blurt out: "She never likes people I meet first."

He disappears like last week's allowance.

He heads across the room to charm my mom. Good luck with *that,* Jed.

The door to the greenroom opens, and in walk two burly guards with earpieces and attitudes. They're glued to Lavender's side. Her mom is behind her. When it's live TV, serious precautions are taken against a Murphy prank.

Surrounded by security and about to appear on national TV, Lavender still manages to look supremely bored. How is that possible? And why does it make her seem cool?

My J-dar goes off. I know the moment Jeremy enters the room. He comes right over to me.

"Hey, Jess. Finally got all the spirit gum off?" Spirit gum is made out of ether and gum; it's what makeup artists use to attach fake hair to skin.

"Yeah, no more cookie duster." I rub my lip. "Hey, sorry about Eva crashing in on us. You had a good plan."

"No worries." He grins. "The worst part was that the mustache looked cuter on you than on me."

As if!

A production assistant beckons for the cast. Keiko rushes to E to give her nose, forehead, and chin some final pats of translucent powder. Without powder, you can come across shiny and plastic on-screen. E looks cute in a loose pink dress and elaborate eye makeup. Keiko hisses a last piece of advice: "Always assume the microphone is *on*!"

Jeremy melts away from me. I see him waiting for Paige and then heading for the stage beside her.

hose of us left in the greenroom huddle around the TVs. Mom is nervously chowing through a plate of snacks. Keiko is taking notes.

On-screen, Genie asks Lavender the first question: "Tell the truth—how furious are you with the success of Murphy's song 'Purple Heartache'?"

"Aw, be sweet, Genie. Who said Ah was furious at all?"

"Aren't you?"

"It's simply a setup for the success of *mah* song."

"Your song?"

"Coming soon, Genie. Ah'm writing the lyrics and will be recording it real soon."

Genie faces the camera: "A Hype exclusive! Now, that's music to my ears!"

Genie turns to Eva, and I can feel Mom's whole body tense beside me. "Eva, is there any truth to the rumors that your *Two Sisters* character is headed for heartache?"

"Genie, if I start giving away story secrets, the next lines I'll read are 'Eva Ortiz, fade to black.' "

The audience laughs, and Mom relaxes a bit. Though she's still eating potato chips like it's her job.

"Jeremy, any word on the big part that you're up for? Will you be heading for a new acting *frontier*?"

"I'm always interested in the right part," he says cautiously. "I mean, I'm not a delivery guy. It's not about dropping off lines. What can I use the lines to do? How can I—moment by moment—create a character?"

"And is there a special someone you're spending your moment-by-moments with?"

Before I can even hold my breath, Paige jumps in. "We're just friends. Events have expired to make people think differently, but we're just *good friends*." Paige winks straight at the camera.

She's pretty enough to carry that off.

How nice for her.

"What do you like best about Jeremy, Paige?"

"He's funny! And funny people make me laugh!"

Jeremy smiles at Paige. The moment feels true and warm—but maybe that's because all the blood is rushing to my face.

"Paige, what do you think of the success of the show?"

She beams. "It's like a dream that I never thought could come true! Like leprechauns or electric cars."

As disorienting as it is to listen to Paige, looking at her is making me feel even dizzier. The current *Vogue* lists patterned clothes and gold jewelry as "hot looks." Most televisions are low-resolution, so tight patterns—like the one on Paige's shirt—start to vibrate on-screen, making it look like she's jiggling in her seat.

Worst of all is Paige's gold jewelry. The highlights reflecting off the necklaces, rings, and bracelets are completely distracting.

A memory stirs.

When was I last distracted by gold?

As the interview wraps up on-screen, Jed sidles next to me. "I'm sorry if what I said earlier failed to validate your unique person-hood."

"No worries." I'm completely myself—all shyness pushed away. "How long were you talking to my mom?"

"About five minutes. Felt longer. How'd you know I was talking to your mom?"

Not the most difficult deduction when a guy is suddenly con-cerned for my personhood. If he'd come over and apologized for acting like a big dumb burro, then I'd have known he'd been talk-ing to my *abuela*.

Over Jed's shoulder, I watch the cast reenter the greenroom.

Postinterview, everyone is relaxed and upbeat. Are Jeremy and Paige especially happy together?

I don't have a clue.

TOP FIVE HOLLYWOOD MISTAKES

⭐ **Falling behind the trend (are you still into Uggs or Chihuahuas?)**

⭐ **Going with the "less expensive, but I'm sure he's still good" plastic surgeon**

⭐ **Lip-synching**

⭐ **Marrying your backup dancer**

AND MY FAVORITE:

⭐ **Getting caught on tape**

Scene 3

Dad decides to join me on my walk with Petunia. The English bulldog is not the most energetic of canine companions—as in, I may have to carry her home—but my slow-moving dog gives me a chance to take in my surroundings, including the things that are hiding in plain sight.

The neighborhood is in its usual state: pristine mansions next to torn-up mounds of dirt. The security cameras are in their usual state: blank-eyed, staring out at the road.

A memory of Keiko, throwing herself between Eva and the camera phones at the Getty, flashes in my mind. Keiko had that freaky intuition about what the cameras were catching.

That thought is followed by the image of Paige's gold jewelry glinting on the screen.

I look closer at one of the cameras outside a neighbor's construction site. I had thought I noticed a strange glow, and, peering closer, I see a golden minicamera perched on top of the big black lens.

A *golden* camera? As symbols go, I don't have to be a Getty guide to figure this one out.

Now my mind jumps to something that I thought when Paige was busted for faking—oops, I mean *acting*—her accident: Even when no one is watching, eyes can be on you. The eyes of the cameras.

My three favorite words pop into my mind: *Gotcha. Gotcha. Gotcha.*

The idea doesn't come with a *click* in my head but with the *schoop-schoop* of a low-pitched siren. Before I can show Dad the gold camera, a Sunset Security cruiser pulls up beside us.

Schoop-schoop. The team has been all over our street since the Golden Tours complaints. The car is slowly driving past when I raise my arm and start waving.

"Jessica?" Dad says, surprised. "What's going on?"

The cruiser stops. Crew Cut peers out. "Need help, miss?"

"The security cameras—some of them—they don't look right."

Crew Cut looks doubtful. Babyface starts a lecture about the importance of amateurs not interfering in an investigation.

I try to explain, but all the officers hear is "I'm a teenager! Ignore the words coming out of my mouth!"

Luckily, Dad heads right for the nearest camera. His gearhead instincts take over, and soon he's prying away. "Jess, you found something. This doesn't look right."

An adult speaking? *That* the officers can hear.

Babyface says, "Please, Mr. Ortiz. Those cameras are private property."

Crew Cut steps out of the cruiser.

Dad explains. "It looks like this little gold camera is piggybacking on top of the existing one. See where this wire is spliced?"

Crew Cut takes a quick walk up and down our street. The golden cameras are only attached to the security systems on the houses under construction—that is, where no one is really living, or likely to notice. He makes a plan. "What if we parked the cruiser in a spot the cameras couldn't see? Then we'd be using the Golden Tours' technology against them."

Babyface moves the cruiser. Dad, Little P, and I hang out beside it for a while, quizzing the officers about their job.

I have to know. "How much is your job like *CSI: Beverly Hills*?"

"More biddies, less bodies," Babyface says.

Then they find out that Dad is a mechanic, and the inevitable happens: the request for free advice.

Crew Cut says, "The right window in the back is making a squealing sound when I roll it down. What do you think that is?"

"Is it a *squee* sound? Like glass and rubber? Or a *scrunch*? Like small pieces of metal grinding?" Dad spends more time interpreting odd sounds than the Varjay School of Acting.

"I haven't heard it at all," Babyface says. "If that helps."

When Dad gets in the backseat to take a look, I follow, holding Petunia. Just like in a limo, a thick panel of glass separates rider from driver. Same setup, different feeling.

That's what I'm thinking when I hear a voice. Shouting through a speaker.

Petunia startles in my arms.

Crew Cut says, "Buckle up." And hits the gas.

Scene 4

The Golden Tours bus whips around the corner. Open-topped and packed with tourists, the bus hugs the edges of the road as the guide screams into the microphone. When the guide spots the cruiser, what he says would air on network TV as: *"Beep! Beeping beep! Beep!"*

The siren blasts on. Dad buckles my seat belt and then his own. We pull out after the bus.

The bus driver—I get a flash of a gold uniform and hat—floors it, *while still shouting out the stops on his tour!*

We race down through the Hills and all the way to Santa Monica Boulevard.

"We're passing the Beverly Hills post office—the only one I know of with valet parking!

"And there goes Rodeo Drive—at only three blocks long, its

fame far exceeds its size. There you can find Bijan—the most expensive store in the world. After you make your appointment to shop, be ready to spend a thousand dollars on a tie and twenty thousand on a suit."

Yes, it's odd to be in the backseat of a cruiser with my dad and my dog pursuing a rogue sightseeing bus—but the weirdest thing of all—*no traffic!* In L.A.! Plus we're hitting all the green lights!

We're not speeding, but we're moving at such a clip that we're soon coming up on Hollywood Boulevard.

Babyface shouts into the CB: "This is car fifty-four. We are tracking a male suspect, driving a . . . kind of bus. A weird kind. It's going right by a donut shop—not the one with the crabby waitress, the one with the extra packets of butter!"

I think I know why it's taken so long to catch these guys.

Up ahead, the suspect is still touring.

"We're approaching Hollywood Boulevard, where you can explore the Walk of Fame. The 'stars' will be at your feet—inscribed on the sidewalk, of course!"

Babyface asks: "Do you think they need me to repeat the description?" Crew Cut's growl isn't much of an answer.

The bus is knifing through the light traffic, but Crew Cut

doesn't give up. Finally, the bus slams to a stop in front of the Kodak Theatre. Jeremy's hunch was right!

"The theater was designed to show off a magnificent view of the Hollywood sign. Step off the bus and up the stairs to enjoy the view!"

Crew Cut hits the brakes and jumps out of the car, with Babyface right behind him.

Dad wraps his arm around my shoulder. Petunia is snoring, loudly, in my lap. Talk about calm under pressure.

The tourists are helped off the bus by a Darth Maul and a Fat Elvis, who have been waiting nearby, hoping to pose with them for tips.

The security officers storm the bus.

The guide tries a joke. "It'll be fifty dollars to join the next tour, gentlemen."

Crew Cut and Babyface? Not laughing.

Act V

**Loving someone is setting them free
and letting them go.**

—KATE WINSLET

I get two text messages from Keiko. One is a link to this article in Hollywood Hype.

> ### *Fill This Space*
> After a virtual star wars, the lead role in *Space Frontier: The Movie* has been cast. Who has received the out-of-this-world offer? If you don't know, ask your two sisters.

The second message says:

> See you on the set.

What? Keiko is saying it's okay for me to return to the studio? Why? What's happened?

I text her:

```
I can come back? Why now?
```

The response:

```
You're the detective.
Figure it out.
```

I do some quick Googling. *Space Frontier* will be an adaptation of a hugely successful graphic novel series. There's no info about who has been cast, but a look at the book covers shows a blond teen—in a costume like the one I saw in a sketch at Movie Makeup. The guy still looks like someone I know. With a bad case of bedhead.

 Scene 2

*M*y *abuela* said she'd be at my house at ten a.m.

Translation to Abuela time? "Whenever o'clock."

I'm not sure which part of getting her hair done, going to church, and gossiping at the senior center makes her schedule wildly unpredictable, but whoop, there it is.

Close to noon, I'm alone on the patio, watching my nail polish dry. (Even with the rush out of the Getty, Keiko still managed to grab us all swag bags; I'm experimenting with the new It Color: Heaven.) Abuela walks around the house to find me.

"Jessica! *Mi corazón!*" She wraps me in her thin, mighty arms. "You're getting so tall!"

No one lies with love like an *abuela*. Am I right?

"*Gracias,* 'buela. I like your earrings." A chain of silver hoops dangles from each ear.

"*Por favor,* take them, *niña!* For your first day of school."

She unhooks them and presses them into my palm. How can I tell my grandmother that her jewelry is too flash for my school's dress code? "*Gracias,* Abuela."

She must catch me peeking at my watch, because she says, "Bah! I am not here at eleven on the nose! *Los Ortizes* arrive *in* time, not on time. I'm in time for your school talk."

"Is this one of those pep talks where you say I actually don't need a pep talk?"

Abuela looks confused. "What are you talking about, *mi cariña?* This is the talk where I tell you how smart, and funny, and *bonita* you are."

Also good.

"Really, Abuela? Beautiful?" Eva doesn't mean to, but she soaks up every "pretty" comment that gets anywhere near us.

"Of course, *linda*! You look like me!"

I got *'buela*'s looks. E got her confidence.

"And, Jessica, it is easy to see how smart you are. Your ideas are the same as mine! Here is my advice: everything turns out for the best for the girl who the makes the best of how everything turns out."

It's Abuela, so I don't ask.

I just say: "*Gracias, 'buela. Muchas gracias.*"

"Now I will bring you to the set." She claps her hands happily. "Your sister has a surprise for you!"

I want to ask Abuela: What's Spanish for *yikes*?

Scene 3

*M*y all-clear for the Banks Brothers studios came just in time. My sister is helping me.

In the name of "help," Eva has cast the role of my imaginary boyfriend and crashed my stakeout. Today, for a change, her help is actually . . . helpful. She's asked Hélène, the fabulous French costume supervisor, to custom-fit my school clothes.

"Thanks for setting this up, E."

"What's a big sister for?"

"Usually? Causing maximum trouble in minimum time."

"I could describe a little sister the same way."

Ouch. Hurts 'cause it's true.

My order from the Lands' End catalog arrived this morning. This fall, no more choosing outfits each morning. I'll be wearing a red, gray, and white plaid skirt, a white top, and a red sweater with the school crest. Every day.

Mom and I placed the order based on the Academy guidelines: "How one dresses is a meaningful indication of how one respects oneself and others. Wearing your school uniform supports the values and principles of Holy Sisters Academy. In addition to following the explicit guidelines enclosed, cooperation with the spirit of the school uniform policy is expected."

Sounds like the sisters have heard *all* the excuses.

There are also detailed instructions like: girls' skirts must be hemmed no more than two finger widths above the top of the kneecap. And a special note that "the Lands' End 'at-the-knee length' chino skort is the only acceptable length. The corduroy skort is not allowed."

Wow. I'm going to a school where a *corduroy skort* is taboo! The skort is always a questionable fashion choice, but a *risqué* one?

"I'm going to hem the skirt a bit." Hélène doesn't come right out and call me *short*—or, as I like to think of it, *pre-growth spurt*—but what else can she mean? "And we'll pull in the waist for a better fit."

While Hélène moves me around like a doll, she and Eva start talking about what a fantastic week everyone on the set had, thanks to the Very Special Guest.

I'm just thankful that my jinx didn't find a way to kick in via remote control. The guest star shot her scene last Friday and escaped the set with her full fabulousness intact.

"She was giving private singing lessons in her dressing room. And you know how Lighting Guy Bob had, like, the *worst* voice. . . ." Eva shoots me a look. "Well, *one* of the worst voices. I swear, after ten minutes with her, Bob could be a contender on *Pop Idol*."

Hélène catches the look on my face. "Oh, you did not miss something special, Jessica."

Do I believe her?

Let's just say they recruited Hélène all the way from Provence for her wardrobe skills—not her acting.

Le sigh.

Scene 4

*R*oman has called everyone to the stage area to make an announcement. To figure out what he's about to say, I put clue and clue together:

⭐ **Jeremy's familiarity with Marcus at Movie Makeup**

⭐ **The similarity between the guy in the spaceman sketch and Jeremy**

⭐ **Genie's question about a new acting "frontier"**

⭐ **The Hype column "Fill This Space"**

⭐ **Keiko letting me back on set (as in, the stress level around here is about to drop)**

Cast and crew are sitting on the floor or down in the theater seats. I'm kneeling between Eva and Paige in front of the Boston Beanery coffee table. The mood is happy and relieved. A place of honor on the set couch next to Roman is reserved for a woman who must be Jeremy's mother—her face looks exactly like his would if someone stood behind his ears and pulled. She's not one of those spooky young-old plastic surgery victims, but she looks as if she physically cannot stop smiling.

Roman claps for attention. "Great news, everyone! Our own Jeremy Jones has been cast as the lead in *Space Frontier: The Movie*!"

A cheer goes up.

"Great work, Jeremy. We're extremely proud of you and will work with your shooting schedule. The Banks Brothers Studios is a mile over the moon to have Mr. Next Big Thing on board our show. We are rushing out the DVD of the first season of *Two Sisters* to take advantage of this news. The network is talking about signing us for the next three years!"

"Congratulations, Jeremy!"

"Way to go, boy!"

"Good work, Jones!"

"It's a dream come true!" Paige notices me at her side, and looks surprised. "But if I'm dreaming, why are you here?"

Craft Services provides an ice cream social to celebrate. The actresses watch everyone else enjoy cones full of butter-pecan-flavored heaven.

I can't get close to Jeremy. Cast and crew are clustered around him, patting his back, shaking his hand, hugging him.

Jeremy's star will shine brighter than ever.

Is that the real reason he's keeping his distance?

Scene 5

*L*ighting Guy Bob and I are not friends, but since we both spend a lot of time at the Craft Services table, sometimes we get to talking.

Usually I regret it.

"My family thinks I'm worried about my new school. But I'm *so* not. I used to be a little quiet about meeting people, but this time it's going to be different. I'm going to charge right in there. It will be great."

"Huh." Bob looks thoughtful, but that could be because he's choosing between a frosted and a cinnamon sprinkle Krispy Kreme. "That sounds . . ." *Brave/impressive/positive!* ". . . like the start of every horror movie sequel ever."

Who thinks Bob was popular at his high school?

Me either.

I decide to change the subject. "Any leads on catching Murphy?"

"Nah. I hope they get him good. That twerp was so cocky. Always walking around like he owned the place."

What?

What did he say?

By Bob, that's it!

Suddenly everything makes sense.

How Murphy has been getting on the set.

How he has been getting past Security.

Even my weird dream about Peter, the mask, and a single key unlocking both doors makes sense: like the Golden Tours spy cameras, Murphy has been hiding in plain sight, using the simplest of masks.

Peter's words to me at the Getty were a key clue: "There are always Banks kids around. I thought everyone knew that."

Everyone *does* know that. That's the expectation that Murphy has been taking advantage of.

I think.

I race to E's dressing room. She looks happy to see me, or maybe just plain happy.

"Jess, I've got the most amazing news! Guess who I'm going to be working with?"

There's no time to guess because I'm pushing my sister out of her dressing room, and suggesting—not *lying,* but certainly *acting* as though Julian of Spilt Sugar fame is loading up on tater tots at the commissary.

Whoa. Even in heels that girl can motor.

Was it wrong to drive my sister from her room?

Ack! Let's debate later! I have the case-breaking clue almost in my hands here, and *no time to waste.*

Haven't we all seen those shows where the detectives can't quite get around to taking a good look at the major clue? If the show is a soap opera, it can take months for them to get the results on the fingerprints/investigate the suspicious florist/try to get *both* of the twins in a room at the same time.

It's not like daytime dramas have taught me nothing.

I fire up E's laptop. It doesn't take long before I'm printing out the home page from Murphy's *Crank Pranksters* Web site.

I stuff the printout in my pocket and head to Security.

"Hi, Reginald."

Reginald glances up from the *TV Guide* crossword he is struggling with. "Hello, Jenny."

"Do you know this guy?" I show him the printout with Murphy's picture. "Look closely, please."

"Sure. That's Murphy."

Huh?

I was so sure that Murphy was brazenly lying about his identity to get past Reginald. I flash on the way my sister tried to pass off Peter as my boyfriend, Heath: "No one had met Peter before—who could know he wasn't really Heath?" Every instinct I had said . . . *waitaminute.*

I have one more question for Reginald: "Murphy *who*?"

"Murphy Banks."

I knew it! Murphy has been pretending to be a Banks to slip past Security. "Reg, there isn't a Murphy in the Banks family! They all have Russian names. This is the Murphy who's been pranking Lavender!"

Reginald might not be as slow as I think, because he says quickly, "Uh . . . I didn't mean Murphy *Banks*. I meant Murphy, who I'd never let on the set. Again. Even if he had lots of photos of himself with the Bankses and lied about his real name. And was exactly as arrogant as them."

"Oh. Okay, then."

Reginald goes back to his crossword.

That's *it*?

A shrug from Reginald?

That's the only reaction to cracking the case of how Murphy has been sneaking on set?

Good thing I'm not in this for the glory.

"Well, thanks, Reginald. Let me know if Murphy does try to get on set."

He doesn't look up. "Sure. Anything for a sister of Jeremy's."

Um? *Eww.*

*A*nd for more on *eww* . . .

I'm walking down the dressing room corridor when I see Lavender pull her foot out of a purple pump. The shoe is oozing with goo. She waggles her soggy toes and peers at her footwear with horror—and something more.

An old prank: shaving cream in the shoes.

I guess Murphy had gotten on set one last time before I clued Reginald in to his identity.

This prank makes me feel bad.

For Murphy.

If the guy had asked, I could have told him: Write your songs, send your fake notes, chalk your body outlines, and substitute your shower products—but not the shoes, boy.

Not. The. Shoes.

Murphy thinks he knows all about revenge, but when I see the look in Lavender's eye, I realize he doesn't know a thing. And she's about to take him to school.

Look out, prank boy.

You have cellophaned your last toilet.

I almost think it's Murphy's screams that I hear—it wouldn't surprise me that Lavender could work that fast if she set her mind to it.

Except the screams are coming from my sister's dressing room.

"Elp! Elp!"

The door is locked, and no one responds to my pounding.

The cries are still coming, and getting worse: "Eek! Eek!"

I throw myself against the door. Nothing.

"Ook! Ook! Elp! Elp!"

There is a large box nearby. It's heavy and clangy, but I manage to beat the lock in with it. The door swings open, and . . .

"Jessica? *¿Que pasa, hermana?*"

"*¿Que . . . ?*" The words die on my lips. My sister is standing on her yoga mat in flowering tree pose. Sitting on the couch, looking small and quizzical, is a bald Indian man. Who I realize must be acting coach extraordinaire Varjay.

Oops.

"Remember when I said I was going to be working with someone fabulous?"

Kind of wish I had let Eva finish that sentence now.

Despite my barging in, she's eager to introduce me. "Jessica, this is Varjay. Varjay, this is my sister."

He peers at me. "The shy girl?"

"Recovering," Eva and I say at the same time. Then she notices the box in my hands. "Whose box is that?"

I look at the box. On the underside, right next to HANDLE WITH CARE, is the name of a certain Very Special Guest Star.

I shake the box.

There's definitely more clanging than before.

Maybe even some crunching.

Oops plus.

We open the box. It's full of broken pieces of little golden statues. One of the statuettes is still together: a small gramophone.

Gramophones . . . Grammys?

These were—*are*—Beyoncé Knowles's Grammy awards?

May as well say her name. Never mind my superstitious deal: "If I don't say her name, nothing bad will happen to her."

That plan? Broken to bits.

I stare at the box. The girl has won a lot of awards. "She was carrying around a box full of Grammys? How egotistical and insecure . . ."

"Jessica, she was loaning them to an underprivileged music school where she's giving a free concert."

". . . and thoughtful and considerate can one person be?"

As much as I love Beyoncé's music, I'm deeply sorry to be the reason that she'll be singing the blues.

Scene 7

I stay home from the set today. Does this decision have anything to do with the article in this morning's Hollywood Hype?

Only everything.

Gram Slam

Two Sisters' Very Special Guest Star, the very spectacular Beyoncé, found that her Grammy collection was mysteriously damaged on

set. Who was behind the
crime? Who knowles?

I can't exactly send the column as an apology, so I spend the
morning crafting my poem to Beyoncé. Question: with all my experience, why aren't I better at writing these?

To ubertalented
Beyoncé,
What could I ever,
Ever say—

To make right
What went so wrong
When I ruined your prizes
For music and song?

I was caught again
By destiny's tricks

So sorry your Grammys
Got mashed in the mix.

In dark times,
Some wonders stay true.
One is the magic
That makes up YOU.

Another, thank goodness,
Is superglue.

Scene 8

*E*va is working out on her mini-trampoline. Mom and I are at the patio table. She is sharing the acronym she made up for why this will be my best school year ever.

Jessica is blooming!
Every day, your confidence has grown!

175

Select how you want to present yourself!
Something special is right around the corner!

"Um . . . thanks, Mom."

"Hey! Don't look at me like that. I was a perfectly normal teen myself once upon a time. Just like you."

She is so messing with me.

But today, it turns out something special *is* around the corner. Jeremy Jones arrives.

My sister says, "Look who wants to turn over a new page."

"Hi, Jeremy."

Mom leaves. I stand up, and Jeremy gives me an awkward hug— like he changed his mind halfway through. Does Eva have to look so amused?

After a couple of subtle hints, and finally a "Couldn't you trampoline on your bed?" from between my gritted teeth, my sister departs.

I fill Jeremy in on the still-emerging details about Golden Tours. They were launching an underground "extreme experience" tour. They started by getting into neighborhoods where other companies wouldn't go, and then onto private property.

They had plans to get even more intrusive. If their security scam hadn't been caught, they were going to try to get right into celebs' houses!

Jeremy does the *ooh-aah* thing about my helping Sunset Security. Especially since there were even more spy cameras found in *his* neighborhood; that's how the buses timed all their drives through Bel-Air's gated properties.

Then Jeremy catches me up on the latest *Two Sisters* scoop: "Lavender is dating that Peter Banks now."

"What?"

"The girl changes boyfriends the way I change socks." Jeremy makes me laugh. Like I haven't laughed for a while. "Did you hear how Lavender got back at Murphy?"

"What's the story?" I knew the ooze-in-shoes was the last prank Murphy would ever pull on Lavender. But how did she get rid of him?

"The Banks Brothers producers decided that a *Crank Pranksters/Snake Bait* crossover reality show would boost ratings for both. *Snake Bait* agreed to move their show away from the *Two Sisters* time slot, and Murphy is off to Australia."

Possibly forever!

Yowch. Lavender does not mess around with her revenge. Forget your silly songs and purple notepaper—that girl will sic a snake on your butt!

I wonder if Peter was involved with this idea. Did he use his pull at the "Bank" to help Lavender get her revenge?

"Is Lavender gloating?"

"She rushed to Nashville to record her version of everything in a country song."

She is gloating. Star-style.

"I saw Peter's brother—Alex? He was wearing a huge cowboy hat . . . that he said *Murphy gave him.*" Jeremy looks excited. "By giving Alex hats, maybe Murphy had a better chance to sneak on set in a hat himself? People might think he was Alex?"

Sounds farfetched as a plan. And hat-as-disguise? That's totally old school. But it's sweet that Jeremy wants to be helpful. "Sure. Could be."

Jeremy has picked up my *Tiger Beat* and is reading aloud. He's opened to the "How to Catch Your Crush" article on page sixty-seven. "Tell pretty girls they're smart, and tell smart girls they're pretty."

I can't resist. Could you?

"What would you tell me?"

"You're pretty smart."

Ha-ha. *Grr* . . .

"Jess, it says here I should be myself. Do you think that's good advice?"

"Nope."

"Nope?"

"It's good advice for *some* people—most people."

"But not me? Wouldn't work if I—or someone *exactly* like me—was trying to catch his crush?"

"Nope. Someone exactly like you would want to appear to be much better than someone exactly like you. At least for a while. Then when the girl is lured in, you can go back to being yourself."

He grins. "Who should I try to be?"

"Well, you're famous. You could play on that."

"Won't I get a superficial girl that way?"

"Sure. But you've got to have the right expectations."

"Which are?"

"Modest."

Jeremy grins bigger and pulls his lounge chair closer. "Doesn't look good for me, huh?"

"I've heard you have some acting experience, Mr. Jones. That could come in handy."

He leans nearer. His arm brushes mine. "But what if I would do anything for another chance?"

Where have I seen that look in his eye before? He's getting awfully close. . . . "You'd do anything? I mean, nothing doing. Or something."

"Or something."

His grin softens into a smile. A mirror of the one on my face. And still he moves his face closer to mine, slowly, so slowly.

I realize he's giving me a chance to pull away. He's not sure if I want his kiss.

Sometimes the boy seriously lacks the detective skills.

So I move the last inch toward him. His kiss is soft and warm and sweetly salty. Warmth flutters out from my middle through my whole body.

The kissing skills? Those he's got.

We draw apart—a little. He leans his forehead lightly against mine.

"Jess, I'm sorry you got caught up in the dumb publicity stuff with Paige. The studio forgot all about it when the *Space Frontier* news hit."

I mumble a vague "s'okay."

He pulls back to look into my eyes. "I'll make it up to you. I want to give you the perfect afternoon."

OMG—could it be . . . ? "The *Sound of Music* Sing-Along at the Hollywood Bowl!"

"Uh. No." He points to a silver mountain bike that he had pulled around the house with him. "I thought maybe biking? You said you missed it?"

Also good.

I get up to go to the shed. I dig my bike out, and Jeremy helps me wrestle it into the sunshine.

I try to catch my reflection in the bike's rearview mirrors (yes, Safety Dad strikes again). I see the girl that Jeremy likes. His kiss still zinging on her lips. She looks happy and brave and like she's about to . . . kick some TV star bike-riding butt.

I jump on my saddle. "C'mon, Jones. You and me. And don't go calling for your stuntman."

"After you, Teasy."

The sun is high in the Los Angeles sky—I hope it stays there. I don't want the day to end. And not just because tomorrow is my first day of school.

I don't do early mornings—except for today, because it's the first day of school, and, sadly, my sister is pathologically insane.

Too strong an accusation?

She's leaning over my bed-pressed face and chirping happily, "Isn't the first day of school the best! The smell of the hallways, the creak of new books! Finding out what the school play will be!"

I.

Rest.

My.

Case.

I just wish I could rest my head, back on my pillow.

I check my clock. As I suspected: it's o'too-early.

"E, I don't have to be up for another hour and a half."

"But that doesn't leave time for hair and makeup!"

What?

"Hi, Jessica."

Who?

I peek out from under my duvet.

182

Hair Steve is here?

In my room?

Now?

I scuttle farther under the duvet, tucking my arms in to hide my *Powerpuff Girls* pajama sleeves. I recognize Makeup Mary by her voice. "And I haven't decided on a palette."

My sister assembled a professional beauty team for my send-off, and has them standing in my bedroom *right this very now*!

At what point did my sister fully leave the rational world? And did she buy a round-trip ticket or one-way?

Makeup Mary says, "I brought these jeweled skirt clips for you. All the kids are wearing them."

How do people find out stuff like that? I so need to get on that e-mail blast.

After a quick shower (*alone!*), I run downstairs. Steve is set up in the library. He gives me a quick but fabulous flat-iron treatment. My hair looks long and supersilky.

He brushes out my hair. "Why such a stiff neck, Jess? You've got nothing to be worried about."

I give him a look. Has he met . . . me?

Mary laughs. "Please, girl, any story you can tell, Steve and I can top times ten."

Has Mary forgotten who she's talking to? I dive in. "Last year in health class, the teacher asked, 'What is the most sexual part of your body?'" I can feel my cheeks heating up with the memory. "In case you're wondering, the correct answer is 'your brain,' and not, you know, what I said."

Silence.

Followed by: "I'm out."

"Yeah, me too," Steve says. "Can't beat that."

Eva peeks over the top of her magazine. "Don't *even* look at me."

That's continuity for you. There are some contests I can't lose.

I'm starting to think Eva's beauty offer, though weird, is kind of cool. That combination comes up a lot with E.

Steve's work is great, and Mary and her silver suitcase of cosmetics are making my eyes look mysterious and deep.

Then Steve says: "Okay, now you, Eva."

Say what, now?

"Eva isn't going to the set today," I remind him.

"Of course not, silly. I'm going to class. With you!"

Question: Which part of a TV star tagalong on the first day of school says "blend in" to you?

That's right: No part!

Makeup Mary says, "I want to blush the apples of your cheeks. Can you smile for me, Jess?"

When I try, my smile feels frozen to my face.

At that moment, Mom appears in the kitchen, still bathrobed and precoffee bewildered. "Oh, my girls," she says. "The first day of school, and you look so pretty." Mom starts to tear up. "I almost feel like crying."

Yeah. Me too.

Scene 10

You didn't think my sister would forget first-class first-day transportation, did you? She had Keiko arrange for a champagne-colored Jaguar. I'm seated between E and Steve in the backseat. Mary is in front beside the driver.

Mom had wanted to see me off too, but Eva convinced her that I would look needy showing up with my mother. As opposed to just my makeup and hair consultants and my big sister.

Mom waves, and Dad hands my lunch and backpack in through the open window. "Have fun, *m'ijita*."

"Dad?"

"Yes?"

"I texted Leo. Wished him luck."

Dad nods. "Of course you did."

The window slides shut. The car pulls down the drive.

"Looking good, kid." Hair Steve gives me a thumbs-up.

Makeup Mary has the good grace to fall asleep as soon as the Jag exits our driveway.

Eva is giving me the hawkeye. "How do we feel?" she asks urgently.

Weird. Deeply weird.

I say nothing.

Eva is wielding her impressions notebook. "What are you thinking about?"

Could you catch me if I ran out of here? Would my hair frizz out in the sprint? "Well, I'm mainly thinking about fitting in. Wondering if I'm the only new kid in my grade."

"That's perfect, Jessica. Everything you're feeling is so . . . *unoriginal!*"

Now I'm thinking about pinching Eva. Is that "original" enough for her? (But I could never do it; Makeup Mary put a lot of work into smoothing out E's skin tone.)

Eva reads my face. "I mean 'unoriginal' like classic, universal."

I whisper-yell at her, to try to keep Hair Steve out of it. "Like you're never worried about fitting in, Eva? You wore a dress you couldn't *breathe* in to impress some singer you don't even know. And look at you *now*! In this car, crashing my first day of my school because you're freaked that you're never going to have a school day again!"

The Jag is stuck in traffic. Go and stop. Go and stop. Stop-stop-stop.

Eva doesn't say anything.

So I keep babbling. "E, you *won't* be feeling first-day feelings when you come with me. You'll be feeling your same old 'helping Jessica' feelings. You can't . . . cast boyfriends for me. You can't save me. You can only . . . be you, saying, 'I'm not in school now. I'm not going back. Maybe ever.' "

Eva half smiles.

Have I hurt her feelings? She looks surprised, but maybe also . . . impressed?

She takes my hand and squeezes.

The car has started crawling along in traffic. I can see the school across the length of a soccer field.

"I have to go, E. I can't be late for the first day." It's hard enough facing the Eyes without being the last person to enter. "I can cut across the field from here."

"I could walk you," Eva offers. "To the door."

We both look at her shoes: Manolo Blahnik stilettos.

"Those weren't meant for muddy fields." It'd be a crime against fashion.

My hand is on the door when Eva says, "Remember: acting confident is a big part of being confident."

"Did Mom tell you to tell me that?"

"It happens to be true." E folds her arms. "And no, Mom didn't say that. She wanted me to tell you to picture people in their underwear. What's *that* about?" Eva narrows her eyes. "Are you saying I sound like *Mom*? I didn't think you were *that* mad at me!"

Actually, if E was going to steal a speech, she'd go to a major motion picture, not Mom. "I'm not mad. I'm just . . . you know."

She knows. "Yeah. I do. Break a leg."

I close the door and throw my lunch into my backpack. Then I peek through the window to wave goodbye. Head bent, Eva is scribbling furiously in her impressions notebook.

The girl always has work on her mind.

Then she holds up the notebook to the window. In huge letters, she's written:

DON'T ANSWER ANY QUESTIONS IN HEALTH CLASS!

I nod and wave.

My feet hit the field. Big fat butterflies start flapping in my stomach. I'm scared, but I'm not stopping.

E doesn't know it, but she *is* going with me to school. So is the rest of my family. And Jeremy. Everyone who believes in me. Everyone who expects me to succeed.

Their confidence is a gift. They sent it out all summer long. And it's arriving now—just in time.

EXTERIOR SHOT: MORNING IN LOS ANGELES. CLOSE-UP ON A FIGURE WALKING ACROSS A MUDDY FIELD. GIRL WEARS RED JACKET, PLAID SKIRT, AND A SMILE.
FADE TO BLACK.

"Murphey's Law"

Written and performed
by Lavender Wells

Oh, he looked the part.
I'll give him that—
With tattoo ink
And a trucker hat.

Rode a roaring bike
Straight for mah heart,
And Ah told myself:
"Well, there's a start."

But any dog
Knows after dark
If you can't bite—
Don't even bark.

Can't mow the lawn?
Don't pull the chain.

Want to be mah man?
Grow yourself a brain.

Pranks and laughs?
Are you man or boy?
Ah got bored with you,
Like a broken toy.

Can't stand losing?
Don't play the game.
If you never grew up,
Don't trash mah name.

Real faith, real strength—
Had he truly got 'em?
Tried digging deep—
Kept hitting bottom.

Now you're no more
Than snake bait, baby,
For trying to take on
A Georgia lady.

ere are three clues to where author Mary Wilcox lives: *Legally Blonde* was filmed there. *Sabrina, the Teenage Witch* was set there. Celebrities Uma Thurman, Matt Damon, and Paul Revere were born there. ;)

Visit www.hollywoodsisters.com for more information.

PSST! DON'T MISS THE NEXT BOOK IN THE *Hollywood Sisters* SERIES

Mary Wilcox

Fashionista. Comedian. Thief?

Brand-new school, brand-new me? Try again. Having a famous sister doesn't make me special at my posh Beverly Hills academy. But I *am* getting a lot of attention. Photos are disappearing faster than MTV swag bags from my classmates' lockers—and blaming the new girl is the reaction du jour. I can't bother my almost-boyfriend Jeremy with my problems—and solving Project Photo Frame-Up is only *one* of them. Convincing my friends that I'm not a kleptomaniac, helping Eva nail her Serious Actress audition, and doing Jeremy a favor that makes my brain hurt? It makes a girl wonder—is a Hollywood ending in sight?

Not. Even. Close.

FADE IN:

INTERIOR SHOT: LIGHT-FILLED HALLWAY. ROWS OF DARK OAK DOORS ACCENT FRESHLY PAINTED WALLS.

CUT TO: PETITE, BROWN-EYED, BRUNETTE TEEN. HER HAND REACHES FOR A HEAVY-HANDLED DOORKNOB.

*H*oly Sisters Academy has a swimming pool, a theater, a student lounge, and tennis courts, but it does lack something: a magical sorting hat to tell me who I'm going to hang out with. *Bibbiti-bobbiti! A cutesy rhyme! Will tell me where! I'll spend my time!*

HSA relies on a more traditional approach: grill the new girl.

The orientation guide drops me off at my homeroom. Six girls look me over. Their uniforms match: red-gray-and-white skirts, white tops, and kneesocks. So do their expressions: curious and . . . judging?

Hmmm . . . the students were a lot smilier in that HSA brochure Mom and Dad fell in love with.

A girl with intense blue eyes and a pointy nose walks right up to me. She tugs at her light brown ponytail. Then—what's up?—she takes my backpack from my shoulder and tosses it onto the long wooden table.

"I'm Rebecca. We're going to be friends, since my previous best friend was tragically turned into a girl-bot. It's a very sad story. You might cry."

"Rebecca, I'm standing right here." A girl with waist-length, curly red hair and freckles smiles at me. "Rebecca likes to tease me about having a boyfriend."

"Don't be fooled, Jessica." Does everyone already know my name? "The Ally you see will be sucked into her phone at the merest text message from her guy."

"Rebecca, stop freaking the new girl. You're being completely . . ." A phone beeps. Ally jumps for her bag.

"She's not even ignoring me ironically!" says Rebecca as Ally whips out her cell.

Now the other girls in the room approach, led by a tall black girl. Her hair is braided in rows to the top of her head, then loose to her shoulders. She doesn't introduce herself;

she does start quizzing me about my old school. "Going to school with boys—it stunted your growth, right?"

"Um . . . I don't think so. A lot of people in my family are short."

"Your *intellectual* growth."

"Oh. No. Not that I know of." The girls look doubtful. Ouch. Boys mainly ignored me, but I'm not intellectually stunted enough to confess *that*.

Rebecca elbows the dark-eyed girl. "Keneesha is a certified genius—except she flunked Remedial Politeness. Keneesha, meet Jessica."

There's a flurry of other names thrown at me from Keneesha's group—and more questions about academics and "the oppression of a male-dominated school environment." Rebecca explains that HSA offers scholarships to some of the most brilliant girls in L.A.

I don't get a chance to introduce myself, because Rebecca does it for me.

Badly.

"Yes, she's Eva Ortiz's sister. Jessica is an amazing actress, plus a phenomenal singer and dancer. A triple threat."

Say what now?

I am cursed with a somewhat threatening bad-luck streak, but as for the rest of the description . . .

"I'm not really like that, Rebecca."

"Everyone knows what you've got, Jessica. You're so modest!"

"No, I'm so . . . accurate." I'm okay on the dance floor, but I can barely act interested when my sister talks about "the call of the stage," and as for my voice? Lawn mowers sound better.

"Another DQ?" Keneesha doesn't look convinced, or especially interested. Her group turns away and jumps into conversation about their favorite reality TV show.

"It's Liver and Pancreas Week on *Real Surgery*!"

A double bill? I'll pass. Twice.

"That's Keneesha and crew. Massive brainpower, minimum contact with reality. Here's hoping they use their powers for good." Rebecca looks at my backpack. "Is that a Hello Kitty sticker?"

"One of the girls at orientation gave it to me. For good luck." I'm not sure it's working. "Keneesha called me a DQ. What's that?"

The door opens and in walks a tall, thin blonde. She's wearing the same uniform as the rest of us, but, somehow, she's wearing it *better*. She throws a nod back at the two girls behind her, who rush to carry her backpack while she checks her lip gloss.

Rebecca whispers, "That's Giselle. She's a DQ."

Somehow, I had already figured that out.